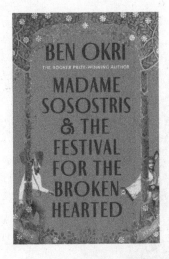

Publicity • kathryn@headofzeus.com
020 30890380

Sales • sales@headofzeus.com

What do you do when your heart has been made a wasteland by love?

Viv had the idea for the inaugural Festival for the Broken-Hearted on the anniversary of the day her first husband left her. Six months later, crowds descend on the grounds of a dreamlike chateau in the South of France, avidly awaiting the experience of a lifetime.

Everyone is in fancy dress. No one knows who anyone is. They wander the beautiful woods with just one night to change everything. And to crown it all, a very special guest is expected for one night only: world-renowned clairvoyant and fortune-teller Madame Sosostris, not seen since the pages of T.S. Eliot's 'The Waste Land'.

But will she actually appear at all, or will Viv's carefully orchestrated festival fall to pieces? Will Viv and her husband make it through the night? Will anyone else?

Part vision, part mystery, this story of a midsummer night's madness is also an homage to Eliot's famous poem, in Ben Okri's inimitable style, as alive with echoes and reverberations as the enchanted forest itself. Hearts will be healed, and hearts will be broken, but nobody will leave this festival exactly as they arrived.

SIR BEN OKRI was born in Minna, Nigeria. His childhood was divided between Nigeria, where he saw first-hand the consequences of war, and London. He has won many awards over the years, including the Booker Prize for Fiction, and is also an acclaimed essayist, playwright, and poet. In 2019 *Astonishing the Gods* was named as one of the BBC's '100 Novels That Shaped Our World'.

benokri.co.uk

MADAME SOSOSTRIS &
THE FESTIVAL FOR THE
BROKEN-HEARTED

An Apollo Book

First published in the UK in 2025 by Head of Zeus,
part of Bloomsbury Publishing Plc

9 7 5 3 1 2 4 6 8

A catalogue record for this book is available from the British Library.

ISBN (HB): 9781035910755
ISBN (XPB): 9781035910731
ISBN (E): 9781035910724

Printed and bound in Great Britain by CPI Group (UK) Ltd, Croydon CR0 4YY

MIX
Paper | Supporting
responsible forestry
FSC® C013604
www.fsc.org

Head of Zeus
5–8 Hardwick Street
London EC1R 4RG

WWW.HEADOFZEUS.COM

Are you sure that we are awake?
                    A Midsummer Night's Dream
                    Shakespeare

Whoever cannot seek the unforeseen sees
Nothing, for the known way is an impasse.
                    Heraclitus

For Judith Gurewich

Read slowly

BOOK ONE

1

THE ROAD TO unhappiness is predictable, but the paths to happiness are surprising.

Viv had the idea for the festival on the twentieth anniversary of the day her first husband abandoned her. She didn't know it was the anniversary at the time.

She had been at a friend's party in Hampstead and found herself talking to a nice woman, a stranger, about the impossibility of recovering from real heartbreak.

'There are organisations for people who grieve, for alcoholics and other kinds of addicts,' Viv said. 'But if you've been devastated by the love of your life walking out on you, where the hell do you go?'

'The million-dollar question,' said the stranger.

That was when Viv had her epiphany. She immediately saw shadowy people wandering about in a well-lit forest and had a fleeting impression of piano music.

'Wouldn't it be great,' Viv said, 'to hold a festival for people who've been smashed up by love?'

The stranger seemed fascinated by the idea.

'You mean, people who've been dumped?'

'Yes. Properly dumped.'

'I'd go to that. Where would you have it?'

'I don't know. Somewhere unique.'

'Did this idea just occur to you?'

'Yes. I certainly didn't have it when my first husband left me.'

'How did you cope with that? What did you do?'

Then it poured out of Viv.

'I didn't know what to do,' she said. 'I drank a lot and had lots of boyfriends in quick succession and hurled myself into my work. The years passed, I met my current husband and forgot about my heartbreak, till today.'

'Odd that you should remember it now.'

'I know,' said Viv. 'But now that I think about it, this is the anniversary of the day he left.'

'Is it? How strange. It must have really hurt for you to have forgotten it all this time and suddenly to remember it today.'

'It is strange, when you think about it. But it did hurt. It still does.'

'I love the idea of the festival.'

'Do you?' said Viv. 'As soon as I told you about it, I felt a little shiver.'

'Did you really?'

'The festival would have to be somewhere fabulous. The Amalfi coast or the Côte d'Azur. A bit bucolic. Like a Watteau painting. Everyone in costume. Nobody appearing as themselves. Wouldn't it be fun if no one recognised anybody else, even the people they came with, their partners or boyfriends? What mischief!'

She talked about the idea everywhere. It bewildered most people. They could make no sense of it.

2

SHE BROUGHT THE idea up with her great friend, Beatrice, who had come to visit one afternoon when Viv's husband Alan was away on business. Beatrice had retired from a career juggling portfolios and now sat on the boards of many charities. They were in Viv's house in Notting Hill Gate, drinking Amarone round the new kitchen island.

'Have I told you about this new passion of mine?'

'How very sly of you. Anyone I know?'

'Not a man, an idea.'

'A passion for an idea, not a man? Isn't that the wrong way round?'

'You won't think so once you've heard my idea. Sometimes an idea is the best thing to fall in love with when men are so disappointing.'

'Disappointed with Alan already?'

'I never said that. I was speaking theoretically.'

'I find,' said Beatrice, 'that when people speak theoretically they're speaking personally.'

'We're not all like you,' said Viv tartly. 'For you everything is autobiographical. Even the weather.'

'But, Viv, what we say about the weather reveals a lot. Nothing could be more revealing.'

'To get back to the point, there's absolutely nothing the matter with me and Alan. We are, as they say, safe as houses.'

'An odd metaphor for a relationship. Makes it sound speculatory, like a bond.'

'A relationship is a bond.'

'Not a government bond, I hope. Those tend to fluctuate wildly.'

'Beatrice, I think you'll like my idea. What do you think causes the greatest unhappiness in people?'

'Money.'

'More fundamental than that.'

'Climate change?'

'Too frightening to be the cause of everyday unhappiness.'

'You're right there. I can't contemplate the enormity of it. Much easier to have another gin and tonic.'

'How environmentally irresponsible of you,' said Viv. 'My god-daughter says the root of climate change is in human history. It's caused by our greed, our desire for more than we need, for dominating others. She says humanity is doomed because we in the West will never give up our advantages.'

'She sounds terrifying.'

'She is. But so's the world we find ourselves in right now.'

'That's why I reach for a cocktail.'

'You said a gin and tonic a minute ago.'

'A stronger drink for a stronger avoidance.'

'So you do know you're avoiding the issue?'

'Isn't everyone?'

'Everyone except my god-daughter. What was the original question?'

'I've forgotten. You distracted me.'

'What's the greatest obstacle to human happiness?'

'Poverty?'

'The happiest people I know are the poorest.'

'Powerlessness?'

'Only a sociopath needs power to be happy.'

'I give up. What then?'

'The loss of love.'

'Where's this leading?'

'To a festival for people who have had their hearts cracked.'

'What on earth do you mean?'

'I'm thinking of a festival where people lose their inhibitions and reveal themselves. Get over their heartbreak and start to love all over again. Wouldn't it be great if we could free ourselves from our pasts and become new people, change our lives and find true happiness?'

'That's a lot to take in. It's a bit mad. Have you told Alan about it yet?'

'No.'

'I thought you told him everything?'

'I do and I don't. He already disapproves of my interest in yoga. What he calls New Age Stuff. Not sure I can take another suppressed sneer just yet.'

'Surely he'd support you.'

'Publicly, yes.'

'Not privately?'

'He wouldn't be exactly scathing, but he'd have that look he puts on when he's not saying what he really thinks. That's enough to finish the idea off. I'll nurse it first and when it's ready break it to him gently.'

'You should have more faith in him.'

'You're right, I should. Faith is a tricky thing. Self-interest is more dependable.'

'Appeal to his self-interest then. I'm sure he can find a way to make money from the festival.'

'You're right. And we haven't worked together on a project for a long time. Used to do that a lot. It's what brought us together, you know.'

'Was it? I thought you'd been together since birth.'

'It just feels that way. We were both raising money to restore the stained-glass windows in the village church. We met at the fête. He was funny and considerate back then. That was before I was in the House of Lords.'

'You make it sound as if you being in the House of Lords has made him less funny and considerate.'

'Maybe the House has that effect.'

'Then maybe this project is what you two need. I'm sure it'll cheer up all kinds of people. Let me know if it goes anywhere. Stephen's expecting me for lunch. You know how impatient he gets.'

'Does he? I never notice. He's always patient with me. How's the magazine doing these days?'

Beatrice got up from her seat.

'Stephen just mutters about it. It would take a magician to work out what's going on in his mind. He gets more folded as he gets older.'

'Not literally folded?'

'That would be easier to deal with. I mean his mind is folded. I can't read him.'

'Maybe you two need a project as well.'

'A project would finish us off. What we need is distraction. That's why I think this festival is such a good idea. We all need distraction. Something we can feel good about. Anyway, must dash. Stephen is never more caustic than when I'm late.'

She encompassed Viv in a hug, pulled on her gloves, and rushed away, leaving Viv to the silence of the house.

3

THAT EVENING ALAN, back from his trip, sat in his velvet dressing-gown, on his favourite sofa, with a glass of whisky on the table next to him. He was reading *Howard's End* when Viv came in and nestled down beside him. He pretended to go on reading for a moment before speaking.

'You only squeeze next to me like that when you want to say something.' He paused, still looking at the page. 'So, what is it?'

'Am I so transparent?'

'When there's something on your mind.'

The grandfather clock in the hallway chipped away at the silence.

'Well,' said Viv, leaning cat-like into him, displacing the book slightly. 'I was thinking it would be lovely to work on something together again. I miss us working together. Those were some of the best times.'

There was another pause as Alan, lost between the ticks of the clock, recovered his place. He read a few paragraphs and then shut the book, marking where he had stopped.

'What did you have in mind? If it's a new business, I simply don't have the strength—'

'Oh no, nothing like that. This will be fun.'

'Are you suggesting business isn't fun?'

'I'm sure Zooms and spreadsheets are bags of fun for you, darling, but I had in mind something that would be good for people and also great fun.'

'You're either trying to make fun charity, or charity fun.'

'That's one way to put it. But what I've actually got in mind is a festival. For the heartbroken.'

'A what?'

'A festival for the broken-hearted.'

'I should think the last thing the broken-hearted need is a bloody festival.'

'A party then.'

'A party's even worse. Can you imagine a bunch of miserable people who've been dumped coming together to make a sparkling evening? I can't. It sounds like a candidate for the most morose evening of the year.'

'I don't agree. There are millions of relationships breaking up every year in this country alone—'

'Don't you have the exact figures?'

'How do you get them? Divorce figures, yes. But heartbreak figures? They must be considerable.'

'Why do you suddenly want to be the patron saint of the broken-hearted?'

'Because no one thinks about them. The bottom of their world has fallen out and no one gives a damn. They try and keep it together but they go slowly mad. They lose their grip on life. It would be nice to help people who're in a hell no one can see. It's a good cause. Anyway, who said anything about being a saint?'

After some ticks of the clock, Alan said:

'Is there any money in it?'

'It could be really good for your business. Give it a human face.'

'Are you saying my company's faceless?'

'Most companies are.'

'Better to have a faceless company than a face like a company.'

'Is that aimed at me?'

'Ever since you entered the House of Lords your face—'

'Has begun to look like a public building. Is that what you were going to say?'

'You look the part. Your face has settled into the establishment.'

'You're saying I look forbidding?'

'No one wants to go to bed with a public building.'

'You'll be saying next no one wants to be married to one.'

'Public buildings don't have a sense of humour.'

'Perhaps they don't. Maybe you want me to wear a mask?'

'I can't believe all this has come out of your wanting to put a face on my company.'

'It has a face. Your face. No one wants to go to bed with a limited liability.'

'Touché.'

Viv's face lightened.

'Darling,' she said. 'You've just given me a brilliant idea.'

'What did I say? I'm always gratified to hear how brilliant I am.'

'It's not what you said. It's what you provoked.'

4

After her meeting with Viv, Beatrice was late for lunch with her husband at his nineteenth-century club on Pall Mall, the Oxford and Cambridge, designed by Robert Smirke.

Stephen was mildly fuming behind his newspaper as Beatrice sat down, having been shown to the table by a waiter. He did not lower the paper to acknowledge her arrival but turned over a page sniffily.

'Sorry I'm late, Stephen. Blame it on Viv and the new scheme she's obsessing about.'

There was a midwinter silence from behind the newspaper.

'I say, Stephen, am I going to be addressing The Thunderer all the way through lunch?'

'Could be worse,' Stephen replied without lowering the paper. 'You could be addressing the latest issue of my magazine.'

'That wouldn't be so bad. I like the covers of your magazine.'

'Do you know what's on the current cover?'

'Not some nude woman, I hope.'

A plump waiter came and took their order and brought them bread and water.

'Did you say rude woman?'

'Nude woman.'

'Have I ever had a nude woman on the cover of the magazine?'

'Sales are falling. You might be tempted.'

'I'm sorry to disappoint you, but the cover this week is much more provocative.'

'Oh. What is it?'

'A montage of bewildered faces. It's about the latest scientific discovery. Most people don't like their faces.'

There was a long pause. The first course arrived, avocado and prawns for him, whitebait for her.

'Is that true?'

Stephen lowered the paper for the first time and stared at her.

'You tell me. Do you like your face?'

Beatrice looked flustered for a moment. Stephen put the paper away and began to eat.

'What a question! Does anyone like their face? Are we our faces? There isn't a day I don't look in the mirror and wonder if the face I see is really me. Faces are so arbitrary. I can't think of a single person whose character corresponds to their face.'

'What are you babbling about?' said Stephen. 'I like my face. I am my face. I can't imagine looking any different. I think my face corresponds exactly with my character. I think the study's bizarre. It's on the front page purely as a provocation.'

'Of course, you'd prefer provocation to truth any day, wouldn't you?'

'What is truth?'

'Not the face, that's for sure. The number of times I've been taken in by faces. Untrustworthy ones turn out to be dependable. Trustworthy ones always let you down.'

'You mean like your last husband's?'

'I'll never trust a sincere face on a grown man again.'

'What does that say about me?'

'You, my dear, have the face of an intellectual.'

'I should damn well hope so. I've done enough reading to deserve it.'

'Do you think reading improves a face?'

'Ignorance certainly marks it.'

'Does it?'

'I can tell ignorance a mile away. Why were you late?'

The stately waiter, puffing slightly, returned to clear their plates. They ordered two glasses of Sancerre. Soon their main dishes arrived. Stephen had his favourite calf's liver, and Beatrice had trout. They ate and talked without one activity interrupting the other.

'Viv has a new obsession. Won't stop talking about it.'

'What is it now?'

'She wants to organise a festival for people who've been smashed in love.'

'We all know what that's about.'

'Do we?'

'She's trying to make Alan jealous. Keep his attention.'

'You think so? I'd never have thought of that.'

'Makes sense, though, doesn't it?'

'He'll hate the idea of course.'

'But he'll find a way to monetise it.'

'Such a cynic.'

'It's true, though. Those two are a pair. When is she staging this festival? And what's it got to do with us?'

'I think she wants us on the steering committee or something like that.'

'Oh, no, not again. Do we always have to be roped in?'

'It's not as if you don't usually get something out of her schemes.'

'What do I get out of them? We're like eternal cheerleaders for her elevation.'

'We're her friends, for God's sake. We're on the board of two of her charities.'

'He's insufferable. There are few more unpleasant sights than a man trying to cover up his class origins.'

'You always seem to get on so well.'

'Do we? People who seem to get on well are usually concealing rancour.'

'I get on well with Viv.'

'You're women. That's different.'

'Is it really? You think we don't hide our true feelings, our resentments, from one another?'

'What are your true feelings about Viv? You're both so enigmatic.'

'Hard to say. Changes from day to day. Anyway. She wants our full support for her latest passion. She wants to hold the festival abroad somewhere.'

'Why does it have to be abroad? What's wrong with here?'

'She thinks it'll be more romantic abroad. Something about abandoning inhibitions.'

Stephen laughed.

'The thought of Viv abandoning her inhibitions is

quite frightening. She's the most inhibited person I know, besides your mother, of course.'

'Are you saying I'm inhibited?' Beatrice said, raising her voice.

'I said your mother is. You even say so yourself.'

'Whenever a man wants to say something unpleasant about his wife, he says it about her mother.'

'You're not your mother.'

'I know what you think.'

'What?'

'That I'm becoming her.'

'Are you?'

'I'd sooner—' She stopped herself. 'As I get older, I find my mother more admirable.'

'So that's a yes then.'

'I like to think, since you bring it up, that I'm becoming a much improved version of my mother.'

'Often to improve is to make worse.'

'Is that a quote from somewhere?'

'Does it have to be?'

'Whenever you can't win an argument yourself, you always wheel in some philosopher. It used to be Schopenhauer. Now it's Kant. Why does his name bother me? And why isn't it ever one of our own philosophers?'

'I suppose for the same reason Viv wants to hold her festival abroad.'

They both laughed.

'Have I told you what her latest obsession is?'

'Yes, and it sounds as if you might have caught it too.'

5

A FEW DAYS later, Alan and Stephen met for lunch at Alan's club, the Athenaeum, whose architect was Decimus Burton. It was down the road from the Oxford and Cambridge. Gilded Athena, on furlough from the broken grandeur of Greece, presided over their separate arrivals.

Both men turned up early, though, by strict chronometric computation, Alan contrived to be slightly earlier. They were due to meet at one. Alan arrived at twelve-thirty. It was something he always did. He enjoyed the feeling of stealing a march on whoever he was meeting. He liked the look on their faces when they arrived to find him already ensconced in the best chair, looking comfortable, nursing a scotch, and reading the *Financial Times*. Sometimes, just to throw people off their stride, he would knock a full hour off the appointed time. This way, when his lunch companion showed up, he would be looking almost bored. Few ever recovered from the advantage it gave him.

He was a little put out therefore that Stephen was only a minute later than him. He had hardly settled himself into his chair when the pale young waiter led Stephen across.

'I hope I'm not too early?' Stephen said smugly.

Alan looked at his watch and frowned.

'You're a full twenty-nine minutes early,' he said, as though he were personally insulted by Stephen's brinksmanship.

'I know. My wife's always late. I'm determined not to be contaminated by her—'

'Sit down, Stephen, and have a drink,' boomed Alan. He looked round, but the slender young waiter was detained at another table.

Stephen promptly flopped into his seat. A bead of sweat emerged on his forehead. Alan had found his advantage after all.

'The reason I asked you to meet me is to discuss my wife's latest folly,' Alan boomed, as he wrote his name on the lunch form with a blue fountain pen.

'Folly?' croaked Stephen.

'Folly, obsession, bee in her bonnet, frog in her handbag, call it what you will, it's all the same. I get dragged along, the ever-supportive husband, when I would rather—'

'Be nursing your portfolios?'

Alan glared at him. He found Stephen's tone oddly elusive.

'Managing my investments is not the primary activity of my life,' he boomed again, looking round.

'What is, then?'

Alan was bereft for a moment. Changing tack, still booming but in a more genial way, he said:

'Listen, old chap, my wife says you're resistant to the idea of the festival. I am delegated to persuade you to come.'

'Persuade me? I'm not resistant. No one's asked me.'

'I'm asking now. Your wife's coming, why not you? It'll be the four of us together, like old times, when we used to—'

'Have argumentative holidays together, with you always making it clear to me how feeble you think intellectuals are?'

'Did I do that? I must have been insufferable.'

'You were.'

'Harsh words to an olive branch, old sport. Where's your classical sensibility?'

'When did you acquire one?'

'Always had one, my friend. It just doesn't do to show it.'

'I just don't get how you can talk down to me the way you do. I mean you're just a ruddy parvenu from Bradford.'

'And you're just a public school tosser from Surrey.'

'You think all that money gives you the right to—'

'Lord it over you? Money gives loads of rights, haven't you noticed?'

Looking sideways, Alan caught the waiter's eye, and turned back to Stephen with a more emollient tone.

'Look, Stephen, we're old friends. Let's not turn this into a feast of recriminations. And we haven't even ordered yet. My wife is very fond of you and Beatrice. We want you both at the festival. Will you come?'

'Where is it being held?'

'Abroad. Somewhere charming.'

'Good. Fine. Okay. Yes, I'll come. Now you have my answer, do I have to stay for lunch?'

'It would be nice.'

'For you. Not so much for me.'

He rose. The waiter hovering nearby, ready to take their order, appeared to be trying to make himself invisible.

'You're not leaving, are you?' Alan said.

'Please send Viv our love. We'll see you at the festival.'

Stephen began to walk away.

'Come back. I apologise.'

But Stephen was gone. Alan tried to enjoy lunch alone.

6

AMONG THE WHISPERING guests in the Cholmondley Room of the House of Lords sat an unimposing woman around whom the party mysteriously buzzed. She was giving readings at a velvet-covered table. People approached with trepidation. But they left bowed, or thoughtful, with perplexed looks on their faces.

When the readings were over the woman mingled with the guests. She rarely spoke. Viv had avoided approaching the table but was so curious about her that she followed her with her eyes most of the evening. When she lost sight of her, she assumed the woman had gone.

'Who was that person giving readings?' she asked one of the other guests.

'Ah, you mean Madame Sosostris. Extraordinary, isn't she? Did you have a reading? She did mine, and frightened the living daylights out of me. Saw things no one could possibly know.'

'Can she be hired for events?'

'How do you think she came to be here? But she's very expensive.'

'Really?'

'She's rumoured to be the power behind five prime ministers.'

'Five? Does that include—'

'Of course. But one must be discreet.'

'So, she's the real thing?'

'Known to be the most dependable clairvoyant in the country. Predicted the outcomes of wars, economic policies, referendums, World Cups, pregnancies, even relationships.'

'Did you say relationships?'

'Yes. They're one of her specialities.'

'What do you mean?'

'She reads the cards and tells if people are meant for each other or how long they'll be together or even—'

The woman suddenly looked horrified. Viv turned and found herself in the magnetic presence of Madame Sosostris.

'I see straightaway that you want to be someone else,' she said to Viv, in a strange accent that could have been Spanish. 'Is it power you want or approval? Why talk behind my back?'

Viv, somewhat flustered, was about to speak when Madame Sosostris held up a palm.

'If you want to ask a question, ask.'

Viv was about to, but the formidable Madame Sosostris put up her other palm and stopped her again. Viv noticed that every finger of the small hand was adorned with elaborate rings.

'You want to start a festival,' Madame Sosostris said in her deep, oracular voice. 'And you want me to be there and give readings to your guests. You don't know where to hold this festival. There's a sadness that won't leave you alone. You are still broken by the rejection of the love of your life. But I tell you something. Many people get power because of something that happened to them. But only a dark power comes from revenge.'

'What are you talking about?'

'You were the only one who did not come to me for a reading. Why is that? You think you are superior to the knowledge I have? My knowledge goes back to before the time of the pharaohs. You think this House of Lords gives you protection from fate? Your fate is already written. You are the only one who cannot read it. Do you know why?'

Viv shook her head in a sort of trance. Madame Sosostris gave a mild laugh, clearly not directed at Viv.

'Because you do not know how to read.'

'But,' blurted Viv, 'I have a degree in—'

'Ignorance?' said Madame Sosostris calmly. 'I know people with ten degrees who lack the most basic understanding of the strangeness of life. Take you, for example. I look at your face and immediately like an open book everything is there. You want a festival, but don't know where.'

'How do you know—'

'People like you do not know what you are doing. If you're not careful you will invite the dead.'

'What?'

'You want to help but you go about things the wrong way. You don't pay attention to your own life, yet you presume to think you can save others. Are you aware your house is inside out?'

'I don't understand!'

'Of course you don't. In your life what should be outside is in, and what should be inside is out. You are no good for the living, so maybe you'll be helpful to the dead.'

Viv had never been spoken to like this before. She stood there in a kind of spell, unable to tear herself away from the imperious presence of the fortune teller. The woman stared at her in silence. At last she said:

'You want to ask me a question?'

'Many questions.'

'One better than many.'

Viv fumbled for words. While she fumbled Madame Sosostris spoke. Viv could barely hear her. Every word sent Viv's mind into a spin. Her mind leapt into a hundred associations and images. Madame Sosostris's voice was even and sleep-inducing. Viv heard things not said and did not hear things said. At last she made a great effort to pull herself back into the present. At that moment Madame Sosostris was saying:

'I know the exact place for your festival. It is in the South of France, in a sacred wood. Not even the French know about it. You will not find it in the normal way. Only a child can help you. The wood is enchanted. People become what they are not in it. Sometimes they are better than themselves, sometimes worse. Things happen to people there and they find the mirror they have been looking for. Everyone who goes there finds the truth about themselves and afterwards they are not the same. I recommend it highly.'

'What is this place called?'

'I told you already. The sacred wood, La Fôret Sacrée.'

'In the South of France?'

'I told you already.'

'I have never heard of it till now.'

'You have never met me till now. I will show you how to get there.'

She had a blank piece of paper in her hands and a House of Lords pen. Viv had no idea how. Then Madame Sosostris, muttering to herself, drew a rough map and made some notes. She folded the paper four times and gave it to Viv.

'I was going to ask—'

'You are going to ask if I will come to your festival and read people's fortunes?'

Viv nodded mutely.

'I don't usually do such things. Now I deal with bigger entities.'

'We will pay you, of course. It would mean a lot to people if you came.'

'You are thinking of the people being in costume?'

'I hadn't thought—'

'No?'

Madame Sosostris paused. When she spoke again her accent had thickened.

'You like masks?'

'Not especially.'

'But I think you will.'

'Yes?'

'All clever people like masks.'

'Do they?' Viv struggled, then she came out with it. 'Madame Sosostris, will you be our special guest at the party?'

'The festival in the South of France?'

'Yes. I will understand if you think it's beneath—'

'Yes.'

'What?'

'Yes. I do it.'

'You will?'

'You must pay the fee I tell you. Business class flights. Limo there and back. Suite in a nearby hotel. One evening only.'

'Of course. Absolutely. What an honour. Thank you.'

Madame Sosostris was not paying attention anymore. She was gazing at the other guests.

'Look at them!'

Viv followed her eyes. She saw men and women perambulating round and round, staring straight ahead. They moved in a blue light.

'Walking round in a ring,' Madame Sosostris said.

'What are they doing?' Viv asked.

But when she looked up, Madame Sosostris was gone. Viv found herself in the blue light. She was among those walking round in the ring, staring straight ahead, as if in a twilight dream.

7

SIX MONTHS LATER, around the summer solstice, the four friends caught a flight to Nice, and drove in hired cars in the direction of St Tropez.

It was unthinkable at this stage of their friendship that they should all stuff into one vehicle. Viv and Alan were in one car, Beatrice and Stephen in another. A tangled memory of a book Stephen and Beatrice had read in the early years of marriage made them take a detour to Cap d'Antibes for lunch and then to Vallauris where they stretched their legs. They were tempted by the waterfalls at La Motte but the shadows were lengthening and they felt the urgency of arriving at their destination before the guests of the festival. Alan drove most of the way and Viv took over at Virgile. Alan nodded off just as they were approaching the precipitous cliff edges of the mountains where the roads wound round like dangerous snakes clinging to the ochre body of stone. In the other car, Beatrice drove while Stephen muddled the way with his eccentric map-reading. He took over the driving at the same time as Viv. The map that Madame Sosostris had drawn for Viv was sketchy and had place names that were not in France or indeed anywhere else on earth. Yet the few recognisable names were helpful.

In spite of the elegance of the landscape they drove through, like most couples, they managed, amid the pleasures, a few awkward arguments.

Many times on the journey Viv remembered Madame Sosostris's hint that they were not going to find their destination in the normal way. It seemed there was a kink in the map. There was a point, beyond St Bonaventure, where the map and the terrain did not correspond. The driving and time did not correspond either. And it didn't seem very much later, though it could have been half an hour, that they came to a small town where the grapes were purple on the vine. It occurred to Beatrice that this curious phenomenon could only be attributable to climate change. But then she saw a child playing by herself near an olive tree and went to ask if she had heard of the mysterious Fôret Sacrée. She returned with a muted look of triumph. The child had pointed the way. She used to play in those woods when she was younger, the girl said. It did not matter much to Beatrice that none of the others even seemed to have seen the child.

They turned off into the woods, followed a triangular route marked on the map which led them to inscribe three sides of a square which culminated in a circle. In the centre of the circle, they found the vast grounds of a château. Behind the château was a lightly wooded hill. Above the hill, the sky was purple and bluish in the falling light.

8

THE TWO COUPLES, fractious and a little worn out by the journey, arrived in a setting that was at once wondrous and familiar. They drove into the grounds in hushed silence. It seemed to them that they were entering a world they had not encountered since childhood.

They arrived with the first wave of festival-goers. This surprised Beatrice as they had expected to arrive long before the others. While finding the château had been difficult for the four friends, it seemed to have been relatively easy for those to whom the festival had become something of a pilgrimage. Beatrice wondered aloud if their own labyrinthine journey had been some kind of test.

And the festival-goers *were* like pilgrims as they poured into the grounds with the humps of their rucksacks, their dusty cars and motorcycles. Those who came by bus had walked the last stony paths from the main road and their weariness was transformed into enchantment when they gazed upon the illuminated outline of the château.

Some had responded to alluring adverts in the national papers. Others had heard about the festival online. There had been much talk about it on the specialist sites. And it was rumoured that it would be a singularity among festivals. There would be no literary or musical events. There would be no authors to pontificate about their latest books or hold forth on their pet campaigns. There would be no famous musicians with fans to fornicate in the woods or trample on the flowerbeds or desecrate the shrines and grottoes of the forest. In what way it was a festival nobody knew, but many had responded enthusiastically to the call. There seemed to be only one qualification for attendance, and it was a mysterious one at that. To admit to the qualification was already to place oneself in a state of vulnerability.

The festival-goers were responsible for their own travel arrangements and their accommodation. Most of them opted to sleep in small tents in the grounds. Those who could afford it stayed in chalets half visible among the trees.

Some of those who made the pilgrimage across the Channel might have noticed the most important item on the invitation, which was in very small print.

9

THE FOUR FRIENDS parked their cars and found their accommodation – two beautiful rooms in the château. They freshened up and met again at the converted stables where the first part of the evening's proceedings was to take place. Viv had arranged for a pavilion to be erected on the top of the hill behind the château and several marquees to be pitched in the grounds. Music systems had been set up. The woods were festooned with coloured lights and electric candles lit the paths. It had all had been managed even better than Viv had envisaged. It was with wonder that the two couples beheld the splendour of the setting for the inaugural festival in the sacred woods.

Soon they would have to change discreetly into their costumes. This had to be done in great secrecy. Even partners were not to know the nature of one another's disguise. The concealment that this called for further strained the couples' nerves.

10

SIX MONTHS BEFORE, as a result of the shattering
encounter with Madame Sosostris in the House of
Lords, Viv had been struck by a series of revelations.
The festival would be for one night only. Madame
Sosostris would be its crowning presence. It would
take the form of a masked ball. Everyone would be
in costume.

'COSTUME?' Alan bellowed when she first mentioned the idea. 'Why?'

'Seems right for midsummer. It's the inaugural
ball.'

'Seems right for what?'

'I'm not sure. The idea came to me after I met
Madame Sosostris. I think I already had the idea but
she pulled it out of me.'

'You mean you were the victim of suggestion?'

'We're all victims of suggestion.'

'Choosing a costume? Such a bloody bother! What am I supposed to wear?'

'What I'm telling everyone else.'

'What's that?'

'Choose a figure from history and dress like them.'

'What? An emperor or a general?'

'Whatever you like.'

'But it will reveal me in the worst possible way.'

'Then choose something that's not revealing.'

'Impossible! Who will you be?'

'Still thinking about it. You do know it's meant to be kept a secret, right?'

'Why?'

'So that the disguises work.'

'You think I'll not recognise you when you're disguised?'

'You think you will?'

'I'd recognise you in a hijab.'

'And if you don't?'

'What do you mean if I don't? I'd recognise you a mile away with my eyes closed.'

'And if you don't?'

Alan laughed.

'Then I don't deserve to be with you.'

'So be it,' Viv said.

'This is a dangerous game you're playing.'

'You think it's a game?'

'What else?'

'It's our inaugural festival. There has to be a ball.'

'Midsummer balls are unpredictable.'

'Sometimes, Alan, I think your brain is your worst enemy. Couldn't you for once just enjoy being a fool?'

'Enjoy being a fool? Only a fool would say that.'

'I'll take that as a compliment. Shakespeare's fools are never fools. Often those who think they're wise are—'

'That sentence is not quite complete.'

'You complete it then.'

11

Stephen was also outraged when Beatrice told him he would have to make a special effort for the ball.

'I run a magazine. Where am I supposed to get a costume? Why a costume anyway? There's enough disguise in life as it is. We need to be more naked. It's all this covering up that's causing the damage.'

'What are you talking about? More naked? What has that to do with hiring a costume?' cried Beatrice.

'Look, it's bad enough having to wear a bloody suit and tie to board meetings. Half the time I feel like a spatchcock chicken. And now you want me to wear a costume? I suppose you'd like to see me in a toga or dressed like an African tribesman, standing on one leg?'

'You'd look lovely as a Masai warrior. You'll need a spear.'

'And you'd be an African tribeswoman, tits out, basin on your head. I can see it.'

'I know who I'm going to be.'

'Who?'

'It's a secret.'

'I don't get that. You're my wife. I'll recognise you anyway.'

'You think?'

'I'd recognise you in a suit of armour with the visor down. And me blindfolded.'

'So confident. And if you don't?'

'I will. How could I not?'

'But if you don't?'

Stephen laughed.

'Then you can do with me what you will.'

'Game on. I'll start ordering my costume.'

'You think it's a game? You ever done anything like this before?'

'I played Beatrice at school.'

'You did *The Inferno* – at school?'

'No, *As You Like It*.'

'Namecasting?'

'You know what school's like. The costumes were pretty lame, though. Everyone was pretty transparent.'

'So no interesting misunderstandings? You didn't end up kissing the wrong—'

'For heaven's sake, Stephen, don't let your fantasies run away with you.'

'But that's all I've ever wanted.'

'What?'

'To let fantasy run away with me. Never lived a single moment of fantasy in my whole life.'

'No?'

'No. This business makes me think about it. Never been in costume before. Never been someone else. Odd at my age, isn't it?'

'Nothing odd about it,' said Beatrice. 'We spend our lives trying to become ourselves. Few people ever succeed.'

'Is that your own line?'

'Could be. But actually I read it in one of your magazines.'

'None of this helps me figure out my costume.'

'Who would you like to be? Cardinal Richelieu? Napoleon? Alexander the Great? Dante?'

'Someone fun. Unexpected. Someone who got away with it all.'

'An artist then. Byron?'

'Too grand. I think the best lives are simple and free.'

'You could come as a fool.'

'Like in Shakespeare? Couldn't do that. Don't want to be taken for one.'

'Fools have all the fun. They get away with murder. Fools have the last laugh.'

'How many weeks will this jaunt cost me?'

'Just one revolution of the sun. Time will fly.'

'Revolution? I hope I don't come back a stranger to myself.'

'We're all strangers to ourselves. It's called the human condition.'

'Thanks for that cheerful prelude to an uncertain adventure.'

12

THE SKY WAS momentarily streaked with grey and a sudden wind made the lights swing among the trees. There were lots of festival-goers about now. They were getting to know one another, pitching their tents, making themselves familiar with the grounds. Their voices were like the cries of birds at dusk.

'Do you know any of these people?' asked Beatrice, as she and Viv made their way to the changing rooms to put on their costumes.

'No idea. They could be anyone.'

'They must be quite sophisticated to come to a festival like this.'

'I guess so. But we've only heard voices so far. We haven't seen any of them.'

'You haven't seen them? That's odd.'

'It puts me in mind of something Madame Sosostris said about these woods.'

'We're not in the middle of a horror story, are we?'

'She said these woods are enchanted.'

'Oh. That gives me goosebumps.'

'I thought you liked enchantments.'

'It sounds more ominous coming from Madame Sosostris.'

'Where are Stephen and Alan? They were with us a minute ago.'

'You know what men are like. They'll be dawdling somewhere, discussing the cricket scores probably.'

'Madame Sosostris said these woods change people. I don't know what she meant, but it troubled me.'

'Speaking of Madame Sosostris, shouldn't she be here by now?'

'I got her a business class ticket and a limo to pick her up from the airport. She should be here any minute.'

'Everyone's excited about her. Even Stephen.'

'What did he say?'

'He didn't say anything but every time I mentioned her he jumped a little.'

'Alan's response was just as strange.'

'What did he say?'

'It's not what he said. He flinched when I mentioned her. Couldn't seem to help it.'

'Do you think they're scared of her?'

'Men are always scared of the supernatural in a woman. It awakens primal archetypes in them.'

'You sound very technical all of a sudden.'

'Do I? Must be this place.'

'Let's get changed.'

13

THE MEN WERE not far behind, and they were not discussing the cricket results. They were discussing their wives and the festival.

'I've no idea why I'm here,' said Alan. 'This is more your thing, isn't it?'

'Is it?'

'Disguises and so on.'

'Why is that my thing?'

'Isn't that what you intellectuals do?'

'Just because I own a magazine doesn't mean—'

'The nation's leading intellectual magazine. Tried reading it once. I felt like I needed to google every sentence. Why can't your writers just say what they mean in a language we can all understand? There's nothing worse than looking up a writer's nose.'

'Up?'

'They write as if they're looking down their noses at you.'

'It's expected of them.'

'Is that why we're here?'

'What?'

'Because it's expected of us?' Alan said.

'When I went to try on my outfit, the costumier who'd made it for me, at great cost might I add, tapped me on the belly and said, "You really ought to lose that." I was so annoyed I didn't know what to say.'

'So, what did you do? I'd have fired him to stop myself slapping him.'

'I did exactly what you said earlier. I looked down my nose at him. Up my nose actually. He was taller than me. You see, Alan, a nose for looking down is what you develop when you can't slap people.'

'Did you hear the cricket scores?'

'I didn't have a moment. I drove all the way while Beatrice listened to a book.'

'What do you know of this Madame Sosostris?'

'I try not to think about her.'

'Viv's obsessed. She's changed since their meeting.'

'I gather Madame Sosostris made quite an impact. She's even got to Beatrice, and she never met her.'

'She's the one thing I'm not looking forward to.'

'I've been dreading it.'

'I've never done this costume thing before. I fear I'm going to make a fool of myself.'

'Me too. Let's get changed before the women make fools of us.'

14

VIV CAME OUT of the changing room as Joséphine Bonaparte. She wore a blue silk empire line dress with a gold-trimmed red velvet overskirt, made specially for her by a couturier friend from university. A mask concealed most of her face. A rose-shaped ruby burned in the centre of her coronet. She looked regal. It became her.

No one had witnessed her transformation.

Viv had done her best to organise everything. She had put in place a team to maintain the smooth flow of events. All she was waiting for now was the crowning presence, the *point d'appui*, the key element of the evening.

Up till now, Viv had always believed in not thinking things to death. She always planned meticulously but once the planning was done she let events unfold as they would. But this time she couldn't do that.

And she still hadn't heard from Madame Sosostris. She had to find out where she was. Phone calls to the number she'd been given didn't go through. She wasn't even able to leave a message.

As she hurried out towards the woods to make some calls, not wanting to be overheard, she had a terrible sense of foreboding which took the form of a throbbing in her head. There were people all about. Some were talking, some were walking alone, some were sitting in groups. A few were lying on the lawn, laughing. Behind them, in the gloaming, were ghostly forms. What was she seeing? They seemed so familiar. What were they?

She passed a white Chaka the Zulu and a black Shakespeare. Somewhere among the trees she saw Charlemagne. Then she realised these were just the guests of the festival, already in fancy dress, and that the ball was about to begin. But it couldn't possibly begin without Madame Sosostris, the star of the show.

A woman in a costume Viv didn't recognise ran towards her, giggling. She was chased by a man in a costume so modern she couldn't place it either. The whole point of a costume, she mused, was that it should be instantly recognisable. Obscurity defeated the purpose. She came to a fork in the path. One track led into the thickness of the woods. The other led up to the pavilion on the hill, shining there in ghostly splendour.

15

THE GROUNDS OF the château were alive. Ghostly forms hovered among the trees, moving restlessly and then vanishing. Music drifted from the tents where revellers were drinking and talking over one another. The music wove its way through their voices, creating a silence of its own and a forlorn mood that was also a happy one.

The guests were now all in costume. Their voices were animated by their excitement. There were cowboys, Mongols, Ottoman Turks, Elizabethans. There were pirates, Moors, African warriors, Roman senators, pharaohs, Aztecs, people of the rainforest, Spanish conquistadors. A scuffle broke out over an SS uniform. Somewhere Lincoln was chatting with Cleopatra, Josephine Baker was flirting with Che Guevara, Mozart was instructing Socrates, Frida Kahlo was seducing Byron, and Julius Caesar was sitting disconsolately with a garrulous Confucius.

And standing under a tree, Pope Innocent absolved Genghis Khan.

When the guests first arrived they had been shy. They'd stayed in corners, watching the tent fill up with outlandish costumes from all of world history. Then they watched the appearance of androids and robots, aliens, folk from other planets, beings from the far distant future and from the farthest reaches of the universe.

Then came the spirit costumes. These were the most amazing of all. Some were elaborate and strange, made of feathers and steel, glass and plastic, gold and bamboo. It was hard to say whether they were indeed costumes or actual spirits. These spirit costumes drifted about the tent and went through the walls and one drifted right up through the ceiling. Then etiolated lights floated into the tent. Sometimes a single light by itself hovered just above the revellers' heads. It would appear to look around and then simply disappear. There was no formal leaving.

Soon those who were alone found that they weren't so alone anymore. There were wonderful fragrances in the air, mingled with odours that were not of this world and which filled the heart with longing for faraway galaxies, for the taste of deep space, like a forgotten lust in the soul. There were many voices and conversations. People who were shy, withdrawn or given to depression and solipsism found themselves in animated dialogue and laughter. Shy women became expansive, and expansive men became restrained and a pleasure to listen to and learn from.

Delicious finger foods were brought in on silver platters by tall girls with long necks. Cocktails were served by men in red suits and platform shoes. A steady hum of voices enlivened the tent. The guests felt themselves to be in the midst of a real Midsummer Night's party in a forest that promised enchantments, in a place in which almost anything was rumoured possible. But for all the hum of voices and the release of inhibition something tempered the mood. Everyone felt under an obligation to behave well and to conduct themselves decorously. Not mentioned or commanded, it was just part of the atmosphere of the woods. They did not want to dis-inhibit themselves to the point where the spirits of the woods would be disturbed. Perhaps there was a subconscious fear that if they disturbed the invisible inhabitants of the woods they might get more than they bargained for.

Anyone overhearing the conversations in the tent might be forgiven for thinking themselves marooned on an unknown planet. Scraps of phrases, overtaken by other scraps, sounded like a symphony of sampled voices.

'Are you here too because you died before your time?'

'I want to get my birth right this time round.'

'Did you hitch a ride from the moon?'

'Turn left at the farthest star, and you'll find my home, nestled in a secret paradise. I left because I was heart-twisted.'

'I heard that the depths of the earth, where the core is as sweet as marshmallows, is where the light we seek is hidden.'

'Do you swim in the honey they call memories or do you prefer the sterner coffee of nostalgia?'

'I found myself here because of an invitation delivered to someone who died of love.'

'How can you die of love?'

'If it's the only food you can digest and in every store in the world it's absent.'

'What is that costume?'

'An afterthought. Do you like it?'

'I'm surprised I'm here, considering how I died.'

'The universe gives us all a second chance.'

These were snatches of overheard conversation. But there were conversations that could not be heard, and conversations that could be heard but not comprehended, because the language was the unbearable language of truth.

'She left me a year ago. I still can't sleep.'

'He left five years ago and I've done nothing since then.'

'They left and took my soul away.'

'I stopped living when she didn't return.'

'I just stare at the wall. People think I've gone mad.'

'I've gone mad.'

'That's why it's fabulous being here.'

'When will it start?'

'I've come all this way. It better start soon.'

'I can't live with this anguish a moment longer.'

The buzz of voices continued for a while. Among the revellers there was an underlying feeling of restless-ness as they waited for the ball to begin.

16

IN THE FOREST, forms were looming. Intimations of past and future events drifted through the tall tropical flowers. Viv, half aware of the forms and thinking them merely shadows, made her call, repeatedly, to the same number. There was no answer and still she couldn't leave a message. She rang and listened and rang again. The phone rang and rang and then slipped into a tonal void.

Viv bent her thoughts to Madame Sosostris, hoping that by some kind of telepathy she could communicate with her. She had come to feel that she had a spiritual connection with the fortune teller. After all, it was Madame Sosostris who had initiated the conversation in the House of Lords. Where are you? You should be here now. You know that the inaugural festival is built around you, Viv said desperately to herself. She rang the number six more times, then gave up.

She made her way back through the broken shadows, feeling hollow. She had no idea what to do. As she neared the old stables, a girl ran up to her.

'*Madame, Madame, vous êtes Viv?*'

'*Oui, pourquoi?*'

'This is for you.'

'How do you know I'm Viv?'

'They said you had gone to make a call.'

The girl handed over an envelope and disappeared into the dark.

Viv stood there for a moment, aware of the fragrance of hyacinths. Nearby, something that seemed like an apple tree was in blossom. The sky was a Morse code of stars. She looked at the envelope and turned it over. She hadn't seen one of these in a long time. She tore it open, took out the paper and read the telegram with a sinking heart.

17

AFTER SHE READ, she fell into a sinkhole in her mind. The stars were whirling and she couldn't make them stop. Her reputation, her prestige was bound up in the success of this festival. Someone has done this to me deliberately, she thought. Done it out of spite.

The stars whirled, but the earth was still. This disorientated her. She walked one way, then another. How could you? she thought. How could you let me down like this? It's impossible. What am I to do? Everyone is here. They have all arrived. They will be expecting the event I have prepared so meticulously.

She could hear the voices of revellers in the main tent. The voices were strange, buzzing, fluting, and sometimes harsh. For a moment she had a sense of something otherworldly about them.

The music seemed to have started, though she hadn't given the order for it. Perhaps the restlessness of those gathered had forced the issue. She didn't mind. The tranquillising effect of music would hopefully keep the guests distracted while she figured out what to do. She did not want to go back into the building. She would feel foolish doing so, knowing what she did, and in the costume she was wearing. I'm the Empress of France, the Queen of Italy, the wife of Napoleon, she said to herself. And as powerless as a slave in Ithaca.

She felt fully exposed by the folly that was dawning upon her, the folly of thinking that at her own command, with a single event, she could make the miserable happy. Who was miserable now?

She was deep in the woods. The fairy lights did not penetrate this far. She thought she heard someone call her name. She had not explored the grounds and did not know where this path went. Still feeling unable to face the others and the signal failure of the festival, she went even deeper into the comforting darkness where there would be no judgement. Then something made her stop. She felt a strange animal presence, and her heart raced at the prospect of confronting a wolf or some other wild creature. When she turned, nearly leaping out of her skin, she saw the shadowy form of a figure gazing at her with luminous eyes. The figure did not speak but only stared at her. Then it held up to her, with a hieratic gesture, a single tarot card. Viv could hardly make out the card before the bright form vanished, plunging the woods into even greater darkness than before.

'Madame Sosostris!' Viv cried.

Then she ran out of the woods, as fast as the constriction of her costume would allow.

18

Nothing like this had ever happened to her before. She had heard about these things but had assumed they were the product of drugs or drink.

She stopped at the edge of the woods, panting. She could see the lights of the old stables, where she had changed into her costume. She needed time to think. Clearly she could not tell anyone what she had seen. They would laugh at her. It was enough that she was interested in yoga and crystals and planetary alignments. Already her husband's silent and very English disapproval of this spiritual interest was beginning to eat away at the edges of their relationship. All the practices she was beginning to explore went against her middle-class upbringing, and Alan knew it. Hence his muteness on the subject. She could not tell him what she had seen. It would have to stay another secret among many.

But what was she to do about the festival? It dawned on her with great force that she had a major problem on her hands, a problem to which she could see no solution. The vision of Madame Sosostris made everything even more difficult.

She hurried towards the building.

BOOK TWO

1

IN THE BUILDING the first person Viv encountered was a man in the costume and mask of a Venetian fool. He wore black tights, a suit of green velvet trimmed with lace, and a tricorn hat with bells. His mask was fixed in a perpetual grin. Without thinking, given over more to the problem at hand than to anything else, half suspecting that she knew the jester, she said:

'It's a disaster!'

'What?' said the fool.

'The whole thing's ruined.'

'What's happened?'

'It was so meticulously planned,' she said, only half aware that she was speaking to someone she did not know. 'All it took was one element to spoil it all.'

'What's gone wrong?'

Viv felt reasonably safe in her disguise. She was sure the Venetian fool couldn't see through her. Yet she spoke to him with familiarity.

'The fortune teller can't make it.'

'Why not?'

Viv choked up a bit.

'Something came up that she couldn't foresee,' she said.

'What kind of a fortune teller is she, then?'

'She came highly recommended.'

'Like all the worst things.'

'Now I'm stuck.'

'But everyone's here now.'

'In their costumes.'

'Eager for revelations.'

'She was to be my *pièce de résistance*.'

'People can't resist a fortune teller.'

'I know. That delicious hint of scandal.'

'Broken dreams.'

'Fraudulent hopes.'

The fool paused a moment.

'What will you do?'

'I don't know,' said Viv. 'All we have are people in costume.'

'And masks.'

'It's a disaster.'

Streams of revellers were pouring down the

corridors, speculating loudly about when the festival would begin.

'Look at them in their masks!'

The Venetian fool watched the festival-goers as they swayed and giggled and talked.

'I find faces more mysterious than masks,' he said.

'They're going to be so disappointed.'

'People in costume are so transparent.'

'They're all excited that a fortune teller's coming. And such a celebrated clairvoyant. Madame Sosostris herself!'

'A migration from a famous poem.'

'Would they have heard of the poem? But they all love a fortune teller.'

'To reassure them.'

'Soothe them.'

'Sprinkle stardust on their wounds.'

'Magic on their hurt.'

'A ghost from a poem.'

There was a pause.

'A ghost? What're you talking about?'

'A compound ghost. In the woods.'

'And they all dead or half alive or beyond death, brought here.'

'Is that a quotation?'

'Not sure. It just popped into my mind.'

'Why will they be disappointed?'

'It's really a disaster.'

'But a highly recommended disaster.'

'She sent a telegram from Margate.'

'Margate?'

'Her husband of forty years just left her. She's quite devastated. She was going to read my charts.'

'She should have read her own,' said the fool.

'Can fortune tellers tell their own fortunes?'

'I know of one who predicted the end of the world. A few years ago. Very serious too. Went to Peru.'

'Peru?'

'Said it was the best place to be when the world ends.'

'Madame Sosostris is the fortune teller to five prime ministers. The power behind the establishment—'

'Where did you meet this paragon of clairvoyance?'

'House of Lords. Where else?'

'It's a wonder they let her in.'

'Power and superstition go together,' said Viv.

'Was she actually telling the fortunes of members of the House of Lords? No wonder they never get anything done.'

'Don't be facetious. She said something strange to me.'

'What?'

'"You like masks," she said in her strange Iberian accent.'

'Is she Iberian?'

'She's from Margate. I told you. But when it comes over her, the accent changes.'

'And what did you say?'

'I said I don't particularly like masks. Then I remembered I was planning this festival. She must have read my mind. So I asked her a favour. Didn't think she would say yes. Adviser to five prime ministers? I didn't expect it for a moment. But she did. It will be something new, she said. Or something to that effect.'

'And then the stars did a number on her.'

'It's a disaster!'

They both fell silent for a moment.

'I've an idea,' said the fool.

'When men say they have an idea, it usually means they've found a way to make the problem worse.'

'So unfair. What's come over you?'

She had asked herself the same question. The truth was she suddenly felt that she knew this man.

'Nothing. Have any of your ideas ever made anything better?'

'In this instance,' said the fool with a laugh, 'making matters worse might be best.'

'How's that?'

'Reversals improve most prospects.'

At that moment, the music that had been confined

to the tent spread out across the grounds. It was not the same music as before. This was a music infected with abstraction, a glissando of moods and suggestions, piano notes tickling the air with a sense of loss, of loneliness, of longing, of eternal hope eternally deferred. They both stopped to listen.

'A party in the countryside without a fortune teller is like dinner with your ex-husband without a drink.'

'You make it sound as if people are addicted to fortune-telling.'

'If there's anything people like more than having their fortunes read, it's having their pasts abolished.'

'Well, you might find my idea intriguing then.'

2

THE REVELLERS HAD spread the party throughout the grounds. The music had transcended its borders. It filtered across the acacia trees and could be heard clearly in the house. The festival-goers wandered about in small groups, talking and laughing, sometimes being silent. They carried drinks and swayed with the movement of the evening.

Stephen, dressed as Toulouse Lautrec, stumbled down a corridor in the old stable building. He wore a top hat and a fake beard, a short overcoat, and a monocle over his mask. In his left hand he carried a cane. The mood of the place had caught him, and the faraway music began in him an obscure intoxication. A woman in armour was walking towards him. She had on a skirt and wore a mask and her hair was pulled back. She walked solidly, the armour giving her force and presence. There was something exciting about her that made him feel a little reckless.

'Have you seen my wife?' he asked.

'Your wife?'

'Yes.'

'Why are you asking me?'

'You look as if you might know a thing or two.'

'Who do you think I am?'

'You. Who else?'

'I'm not sure I like your tone.'

'Who are you?'

'Is it not obvious?'

'Not exactly.'

'I'm Joan of Arc.'

'You bear no resemblance to her at all.'

'You know what she looked like?'

'What I mean is, who are you underneath?'

'Underneath what?'

'The costume.'

'That's very rude.'

'I wasn't alluding to your body, madame,' said Toulouse Lautrec.

'I didn't think you were, but now you have.'

'Have what?'

'Alluded to it.'

'To your nakedness?'

'Now you've managed to be even ruder,' said Beatrice.

'I have no idea what you mean.'

'Don't you?'

'Perhaps my persona is affecting my personality. I'm not normally rude.'

'You should be standing on one leg.'

'I don't follow.'

'I mean, that was a lame excuse you made.'

'I've no idea what's come over me. I'm just trying to find my wife.'

'That's an odd way to find a wife.'

'How do you mean?'

'Asking every passing woman what she's like underneath.'

'I believe you misheard me.'

'How charming! First you mislay your wife and now you're telling me I misheard you. Look, monsieur, just because you're dressed as Toulouse Lautrec doesn't give you the right to act like him.'

'How did he act?'

'You know perfectly well how he acted.'

'I still have no idea what you're talking about.'

'All those pictures of women kicking their legs in the air.'

'Madame, is it possible you're mistaking me for the person I appear to be?'

'Now you're telling me I'm not entering the spirit of the party. That does it!'

She gave Stephen a resounding slap. It was like being slapped by lightning. Then she turned and stormed back down the corridor.

'My persona seems to be working,' Stephen said to himself. 'Now let's see what other mischief I can get up to.'

He went outside and into the woods.

3

ALAN CAME INTO the corridor just as Beatrice in her armour was leaving. Without thinking, he stood before her and jingled the bells on his head.

'We've been looking for you,' he said.

'Am I hard to find?'

'As a matter of fact, you're not.'

'No?'

'I recognised you right away.'

'Before I said a word? Am I so transparent?'

'No, not at all. You're very opaque.'

'Then how did you recognise me?'

'Your very opaqueness gave you away.'

'I'm in no mood for jokes.'

'Jokes?'

'I've been insulted enough already. What did you mean?'

'Most people can't recognise people they know in costume.'

'Why not?'

'Because they're too familiar.'

'That's ridiculous.'

'Not at all. When we see someone we know in an unfamiliar context, we don't recognise them at first, even if they're not disguised.'

'Now you're opaque.'

'I'll give you an example.'

'Don't. Examples just complicate things. Didn't someone say that to Kant?'

'I'm not Kant. And I won't speak cant either.'

'God, that's lame,' said Beatrice.

'My example will be taken from ordinary life.'

'Hah! Ordinary life?'

'We're talking in ordinary life,' replied Alan.

'Two people, in ridiculous costumes, from two different centuries, having a pointless conversation, somewhere in the South of France? That hardly qualifies as ordinary life.'

'You're quite right. But that wasn't the example I meant to give.'

'Your examples are multiplying like pickpockets at a flea market.'

'Strange metaphor. But forgivable. You're not yourself.'

'What do you mean I'm not myself?'

'It's self-evident.'

'Are you by any chance suggesting I'm drunk?'

'Are you?'

'Of course not, you fool,' said Beatrice.

'Glad to hear it.'

'What did you mean then?'

'I mean you're in another persona. You're someone else.'

'I'm exactly myself.'

'So, you're most yourself when you're someone else? Fascinating. I'll think about that at my leisure.'

'Do you take leisure?'

'I allow myself to be taken at leisure.'

'I mean do you take time off. By the way, did you mean to be louche?'

'Never louche, my lady.'

'Pleased to hear it.'

Revellers were drifting past them looking forlorn and a little lost. They were all dressed up and ready for the ball, but they appeared to have no particular destination in mind. The music sounded distant and disconsolate, like something heard through a gauze of sorrow.

'If I may slip back to my example,' said Alan. 'I was in Posillipo a few years ago, and I saw a man I thought I knew. He was in a yacht. I was in another boat.'

'I didn't think you were walking on water.'

'As I stared at him, trying to place him, he fell into the sea.'

'You're giving yourself airs, sir.'

'Airs?'

'You're suggesting that your powerful stare tipped him into the sea.'

'No,' said Alan. 'Two things – my staring at him, his pitching into the sea – these were unrelated acts. They were merely, what would you say? Contingent.'

'I'm hoping something followed the contingency.'

'I jumped into the sea and rescued him.'

'Now you're posing as a hero. You were not yourself.'

'Quite right. I was not myself. I was a fool.'

'Your words.'

'I soaked my new suit, my passport, and wallet. Also, I'm a poor swimmer.'

'You've slipped roles. Now you're the clown in the bay of Naples.'

'My finest role, which I commemorate with my present outfit.'

'I wondered about that,' said Beatrice, looking him over.

'What?'

'The outfit. What exactly are you?'

'A Venetian fool.'

'Not Neapolitan?'

'I wasn't a clown then.'

'That's not altogether true.'

'So I look the part?'

'Clad in motley?'

'Yes.'

'I'd never have guessed you were meant to be a Venetian fool.'

'Why not?'

'You look as if you're in borrowed rags. I took you for a beggar.'

'Very noble of you to have such an amusing conversation with a beggar. Do you do it often?'

'My whole life is spent with beggars of one kind or another.'

'You must be one of life's great saints.'

'Are you ever going to finish your story?'

'One should never leave stories or women hanging.'

'You hang women?'

'It was a figure of speech.'

'Hard to figure. Are you addicted to diversions?'

'Diversions?'

'You never get to the point. You never finish a story. How did you make it through school?'

'I never made it through school.'

'That explains a lot.'

'I sailed through school.'

'Back to your boat metaphor.'

'I take your hint.'

'Well?'

'After I got the poor fellow ashore, and got a fish out of his mouth—'

'*Très drôle.*'

'After I resuscitated him, he sat up and thanked me. That's when I realised who he was.'

'Are you going to make an epic of this? Will Agamemnon sail into it? Will a masked chorus sing? Spit it out. Who was he?'

'My bank manager.'

'That's disappointing.'

'*Pourquoi?*'

'Beggars saving banks? Isn't that what's behind most of our problems now? Shouldn't it be the other way round?'

'He was a bank manager, not a bank.'

'It's symbolic.'

'Besides, I wasn't dressed as a beggar at the time.'

'But you are now.'

'That's a strange transference,' said Alan.

'Is it? You don't think the teller infects the tale?'

'Are you implying a sort of magic?'

'Whatever. Now, can you remind me what your point is? I feel you're leading me to Timbuktu.'

'My point is how unfamiliar people seem when

they are in unfamiliar circumstances. Take you, for example.'

'Me?'

'You're in an unfamiliar costume, yet you come across quite plainly as yourself.'

'I've never been described as plain before. Not to my face. I'll not have it.'

She slapped him and rained blows on him. Alan, the fool, made no attempt to defend himself.

'It was not my intention to be rude,' he cried. 'I'm not normally like this. I think it's my costume, or this place. I'm not myself.'

'I don't know you. You're a complete stranger,' Beatrice said, flouncing off in her armour.

'I have no idea who you are anymore either,' Alan said to her absent form. 'I was just going to ask you to stand in for the fortune teller.'

4

THE REVELLERS WERE growing steadily more restless. The music pouring from the loudspeakers was beginning to lack conviction. Food was brought but the guests ate listlessly. They drank and their voices grew louder. A feeling of mutiny was spreading.

Viv, disguised as Joséphine, went among the guests. She asked them why they were restless and if they were dissatisfied. To her surprise, they were friendly and thoughtful. It turned out they were not really mutinous. They were simply anxious to see the legendary fortune teller. They were all hungry to meet her. And they were friendly to Viv who they took for a reveller like themselves. They were full of praise for the organisers of the event. They had all been in deep funks, stuck in the pit of their lives, unable to emerge or move forward, till this festival came along.

They didn't know that she was the person who had put it all together. They simply thought that she was one of them, one of their heartbroken number. Everyone she met opened up to her in a way that was almost overwhelming.

'We love your costume,' said one.

'It's the grandest we've seen all evening,' said another.

'You must have a great imagination,' said a third.

'You've got such a glowing aura,' said a fourth.

'They say Joséphine was more fun than old Boney,' said a fifth.

Viv had never encountered this kind of warmth before. At one point she feared her mascara would run. She thought people were having her on, that they knew who she was and were pretending not to, that their warmth was all fake. But she soon realised that the things they were saying were genuine, that they wanted nothing from her, and had no idea who she was. This was disquieting and charming in equal measure. Disquieting because she was used to people reacting to her because of her money. She was used to the influence of her position in society, the power it gave her. Being liked without that power was new to her. But it did not alter her anxiety.

She was contemplating what to do next when

she saw a woman in the armour of Joan of Arc and waved her over. The friends recognised each other immediately. Complicity grew between them. The music had started again. It was a new music of voices and sweet laments, poignantly sounding over the honeysuckle air.

'It's a disaster,' Viv sobbed. 'A complete disaster.'

'I agree,' cried Beatrice. 'I've been insulted twice.'

'Insulted?'

'For being who I am, and for being who I'm not.'

'Poor you!'

'Something about adopting a persona brings out the worst in people.'

'I've not found that.'

'No?'

'People have been nice to me today because they don't know who I am. Actually, they've never been nicer.'

'That's hard to imagine.'

'Maybe I should keep this persona forever. Much better not being myself.'

'Can you ever not be yourself?'

'People saw me differently. So I was different.'

'Even when you were exactly the same?'

'Precisely. I talked the same way. My ideas hadn't changed. But people were nicer to me because they didn't know who I was.'

'Maybe they were different because you were different.'

'You think so? It was like taking a holiday from me. Always wanted to do that. Are you not fed up with being the same person day after day?'

'And night after night. I'm the same, even in my dreams.'

'It was amazing to be this new person. Liberating.'

'Like being in love.'

'Not like being in love. Like being loved. Suddenly you feel fascinating.'

'The charm of new love,' Beatrice said. 'Being seen completely differently by someone.'

'We get to be a new self.'

'A new person. Who knows how many incarnations are languishing in us?'

'Suppressed in us.'

'It's funny to hear you say that,' said Beatrice, looking closely at her friend.

'If I'm honest,' said Viv, 'I feel I've never been allowed to be myself, not in all my life.'

'No?'

Viv took Beatrice by the arm and led her to a set of chairs on the grass. She didn't speak for a moment. The music of Debussy, distorted slightly as if passing through water, drifted over from the woods.

'They clamp a personality on you,' continued

Viv, 'and ever afterwards you can't escape. If you're known as the grande dame of charities, that's how you'll be perceived long after your bones are bare and white. If you're known for efficiency, you're never allowed to be playful. If you're strong, you're never allowed to be vulnerable. It's like a prison. You're stuck with whatever vices or virtues your reputation has calcified around you. Don't you long to be the opposite of what people think you are?'

Beatrice was stunned.

'I've never really thought about it. People think I'm safe, a sort of modern version of a home counties lady and they say it's quite—'

'It's like being in prison,' Viv went on. 'You're stuck in this idea that others have of you. Once, when I tried to be different, to be how I really am, I could see the look on Alan's face. "But darling," he said, "that's so not like you." I tell you, being someone else has been the best thing about this whole experience. The only trouble is, now it's a complete disaster.'

'You keep saying that.'

'But it is. Can't you see?'

'In my experience,' said Beatrice, 'few things are real disasters. When my first husband got some girl pregnant I thought it was a real disaster and my life was over—'

'I never knew about that.'

'It's not something you broadcast. People would think there's something's wrong with you.'

'Something wrong with him, you mean.'

There was a pause, then Beatrice spoke again.

'It was the most devastating thing that ever happened to me. He was the true love of my life, you know. I never knew anything could hurt so much. It was worse than dying.'

There was another pause.

'Time passed,' went on Beatrice, 'I don't know how, but it passed. The baby was born, and my husband revealed himself to be a pathetic little provincial man after all, and I wished him all the luck in the world.'

'How generous you are,' said Viv.

'Am I? And was it such a disaster? I don't think so anymore.'

'Why not?'

'My heart broke into a thousand pieces and I discovered what you discover when your heart breaks.'

'Which is?'

Beatrice gave a short laugh.

'Life is dead. Long live life.'

'You mean you discovered life after death,' said Viv.

'You're looking at someone who has literally risen from the grave.'

'You look very good on it.'

'If you survive, life after death is the most regenerating experience. I had to go through fire to find that out.'

'But your first husband was a fool. What I'm talking about is a real disaster.'

'What? Not Alan?'

'Alan? Oh, that's another story.'

'For God's sake, what then?'

'Beatrice, what are we women most interested in?'

'Handbags? Sex?'

'Seriously.'

'The future?'

Viv looked at her in silence for a moment.

'That's what I've always liked about you.'

'What?'

'You say the truth everyone conceals from themselves.'

'Do I?'

'Absolutely,' said Viv.

'I just said the opposite of what was in my mind.'

'It's not what was in your mind that counts, it's what you said.'

'I was being perverse.'

'Perversity often speaks truth.'

'But I was just playing.'

'Sometimes play is prophecy.'

'I get the feeling I'm being dragged into something.'

'What if we are all suppressing, within ourselves, many personalities?'

'That sounds almost bipolar.'

'Be serious.'

'I am serious.'

'How would you like to be the saviour of the festival?'

'How could I be the saviour of anything?' cried Beatrice in alarm.

'Why not?'

'Look at me!' Beatrice's voice was still rising. 'I'm clumsy. I upset people. And I'm touchy. People run away from me.'

'That's not because of who you are. It's how you're seen.'

'How am I seen?'

'Right now you're under the aegis of Mars,' said Viv flatly. 'War shines from your brow. Your persona has invaded your personality.'

'What?'

They were sitting close to each other, with the scent of mimosa and gardenias on the air. The music had changed again. It was still Debussy, but the notes sounded farther and farther apart, as though the instrument on which the pianist played was becoming larger and longer. A cool breeze blew through the trees. Viv thought for a moment that she could discern forms in the wind. But when she blinked they were gone.

'Can I be honest?'

'I value honesty more than all the great wines of France,' said Beatrice passionately.

'That's an odd thing to say.'

'Be honest with me.'

'Personality is a construct which we mistake for the real thing.'

'Do you really think so?'

'Yes, absolutely.'

'But that's not how most people see it.'

'I know.'

'In our world, we treat the personality as the person. We don't distinguish the person from the personality they project. Public life is founded on this.'

'Public life is a sham.'

'But life doesn't get more public than you. Didn't you just present a bill for the Protection of Public Waterways?'

'That's how I know what I'm talking about.'

There was another pause. Beatrice seemed a little distressed by what she was hearing.

'What we call personality,' Viv continued, seeing again the forms that seemed to be coalescing and dissolving in the wind, 'is merely a well-rehearsed performance, a habit. Players strutting upon the stage. If you look closer, you'll see that personalities are hollow vessels.' She gave a tinkle of a laugh. 'I've seen the great men of our times rehearse their personalities in the mirror. And a few great women too. I've knocked on the door of Personality and been shocked at the tiny person who opened it. Most personalities are mixed dishes – a bit like my metaphors – cobbled together.'

'What about consistency?'

'Mere proof of the victory of the performance.'

Beatrice regarded her friend as if from a distance. 'You can't mean all that. Are you – disillusioned?'

'I'm not disillusioned. I've just got a new perspective.'

'Explain.'

'It's very rare to find the real person in a person.'

'What do you mean?'

'I mean what's truest in us, most vulnerable.'

'What? Consciousness? Soul? What people really are?'

'Call it whatever you want. But it's not the bundle of gestures and eccentricities we call personality. You look shocked.'

'I am shocked,' Beatrice said, her voice strained. 'All these years I've thought of you as the pillar of society, the consummate insider.'

'Dead phrases.'

'And now you reveal yourself to be—'

'A realist?'

'You call that realism?'

'Yes. It's about what's real, not fake. Society is run on the fake.'

Beatrice winced.

'You know this in your heart,' Viv said calmly.

'Are you sure?'

Viv laughed, her eyes again seeking out the forms she had glimpsed in the wind.

'We play the world's game because we must. We're in this world and there is no other. We may as well play the stupid game everyone else plays. But we don't have to be taken in by it. We can look below the surface.'

'Someone else said that to me today. I didn't take it well.'

'I'm sure you were true to how you felt.'

'It's a little unnerving talking about truth in fancy dress.'

'Maybe it's the only way we can speak truth. Joan of Arc, will you save the party?'

'Me? How?'

'Let's turn disaster into a game. We'll deal with the others. My dear friend, do you trust me?'

BOOK THREE

1

THE NIGHT WAS deeper. In the woods the revellers were gathering. A music of desolation and seduction followed them there. They had been wandering the château grounds and were coming together now with urgency because of the news that had been filtering through to them. Beneath the costumes their distress could be sensed. They used their hands first, making gestures in place of words, gestures of desperation and of a hope that was fluttering away with the night. When they began to speak it was as if the words were pouring out of a dam, fast, urgent, overflowing. Sometimes they all spoke at once, so it was impossible to discern who was speaking, and it appeared as if they were all speaking to one another out of their own need and despair.

'Apparently there isn't going to be a fortune teller,' said a guest.

'Madame Sosostris isn't coming?' asked another.

'She isn't coming,' said a third.

'I was looking forward to her more than anything. What happened?'

'Something she couldn't foresee.'

'Perhaps there was something in her cards.'

'Whatever it is, she's definitely not coming.'

'I've always wanted to have my fortune told and I could never bring myself to do it in England. This has ruined the night for me.'

'We may as well go home.'

'Wherever home is.'

'In the dark or sacred woods.'

'Having one's future untold is death's secret thrill.'

'Especially if one is anonymous.'

'Our lives are murky. We live in uncertainty.'

'I want to peer into the past.'

'The past is the future, the future is the past.'

'I want to know if I'm happy.'

'I want to know if I've already met the love of my life.'

'I want to know if my schemes have succeeded.'

'I want to know what my past holds, so I can prepare for it.'

'I fear the past. I don't want to know the past. It comes soon enough.'

'There is no need to worry,' said someone.

'Madame Sosostris isn't coming so we'll have to do without that terrible knowledge.'

'We'll have to do without the ambiguity of knowing and not knowing, fearing and desiring what we fear.'

'If the cards tell of disaster, don't we secretly want that?'

'If the cards tell of death, don't we secretly deserve it?'

'Our futures are changed by being told.'

'Our pasts are changed by being predicted.'

'It's dangerous to play with destiny.'

'It's dangerous to play with the threads of life.'

'Everything we do is playing with destiny.'

'Coming to this party is playing with destiny.'

'You could meet someone whose touch turns your death upside down.'

'How many of us here will return the way we came?'

'Making a decision is playing with the threads of fate.'

'Not making a decision is letting the threads of fate play with you.'

The three who spoke were vague and formless. Their voices flickered like flames in the breeze. They spoke softly, urgently, as if only desire mattered. The wind swept the voices through the woods.

'Can you remember what it said in the small print, on the invitation?'

'The most important thing?'

'It said: "Madame Sosostris, famous fortune teller, will be present."'

'That's why most of us are here.'

'We want to change our deaths.'

'But don't have the courage.'

'We need a sign.'

'We're here because we want a different death from the one we had.'

'If we have a different death, we'll have a different life.'

'Death changes life.'

'Let's not talk about life.'

'Just the thought of sunlight makes me giddy.'

'That's why we're in costume.'

'And masks.'

'That's why we drink and dance.'

'And talk about other people's deaths.'

'Why we do nothing.'

'And everything.'

'Dream in despair.'

'Busy as flies.'

And while they spoke the piano insinuated itself into their voices. And when they stopped speaking the piano insinuated itself into their silence.

2

WANDERING ABOUT IN the grove of acacias, sycamores and oaks, chased by forms that emerged from
the trees, by revellers who became people he had once
known, Alan stumbled into a clearing and found a
woman sitting there. She was dressed like a queen and
was regal in her bearing. Her presence brought him
back to himself. He straightened up, swaying slightly.

'Sorry to bother you,' he said.

The woman remained noble and silent.

'I can leave if you prefer.'

She did not respond.

'I was lost in the forest. Every path seemed to mul-
tiply and led me back to the same place. I couldn't
escape. I feel dizzy.'

The woman remained silent and still.

'I saw, among the trees, faces of people I've
wronged. Is that normal? Am I in hell?'

'If you are, then I must be the queen of the night,' the woman said, barely moving.

'Who are you?'

'Are you interested?'

'I wouldn't ask if I wasn't.'

'Are you really interested in anything apart from yourself?'

'What?'

'Why do you think you've seen the faces of people you wronged?'

'Something to do with the woods. Someone said they were... but I don't believe it. If I did, what else would I end up believing?'

'Your past follows you. Your truth clings to you—'

'My truth?'

'Have you ever done anything good for anyone in your life?'

'What?'

'Da: Dharma. Who have you helped?'

'You're speaking in tongues. Are you here for the festival? Are you wearing a costume?'

'No.'

'Who are you?'

The woman turned so he could see her in silhouette. Something about her stopped him coming nearer. He stood there in a half trance.

'Who are you?'

'Madame Sosostris sent me to ask you something.'

'Does this mean she's definitely not coming?'

'It depends on your answer.'

There was a pause while Alan considered the courses of action open to him. He realised there was no escape.

'What do you want to know?' he asked meekly.

'If she is unable to come to the party tonight, will you take her place?'

'What?'

'Would you consent to take her place?'

'How can I take her place? I'm a man, she's a woman—'

'So what? Men have been women, and women men, since the beginning of time.'

'But I can't be a woman!'

'Why not? You've been a woman several times before.'

'Have I?'

'Madame Sosostris has studied your charts and seen your past incarnations. She says you're struggling with the women in you.'

'What nonsense!' roared Alan. 'There are no women in me.'

'Oh, yes, there are, just as there are men in me.'

'You can have as many men in you as you want, but don't put any women in me.'

'Do you fear women?'

'Of course not!' shouted Alan again.

'Then why are you afraid to take Madame Sosostris's place?'

'Because it would be inappropriate. Because I don't have her abilities. Also, what would people think if they saw me?'

'You mean your business associates?'

'My reputation would never recover if it got out that I was pretending to be some batty old lady—'

'It could be the making of you.'

'You think I'm not made already?'

'Not by a long shot.'

'Did she see that in my charts? The woman scares me.'

'Batty? Old? Have you ever met Madame Sosostris?'

'No, but she must be batty.'

'Old?'

'She must have been batty for a long time to be like she is.'

'Like what?'

'Making all those claims with a bold face.'

There was another long pause during which the woman stayed very still.

'So, you won't take Madame Sosostris's place?'

'It would ruin my business.'

'It might save it.'

'I don't believe that for a second. I'll take the risk.'

'In that case, please keep this little encounter to yourself.'

The woman had barely finished speaking when she rose, turned her back on him, and walked rapidly away into the forest.

'Wait!' Alan called, hurrying after her. 'Where did she go?'

He rustled about in the woods.

'I can't find her,' he said to himself. 'She's vanished. Was she real? I'd better find my wife.'

He went on wandering among the trees.

3

THRASHING THROUGH THE grove of sycamores and acacias and oaks, struggling with imaginary brambles and shoving his way through resistant vines, Stephen crashed into the clearing and fell flat on the ground.

He had been hurrying away from people he'd glimpsed in the woods. People with the faces of those he had betrayed, those he had wounded, those whose reputations he had destroyed over the years. One of them was a woman who had tried to kill herself because of hints of incest in an article in his magazine. He had glimpsed her among the trees and knew she was after him and so he had started running and was still running when he fell in the clearing.

As he picked himself up and dusted himself down he saw there was a woman already sitting in the centre of the clearing. Her head was turned away from him. She was wearing the elaborate white wig of a judge.

'Sorry. I didn't know anyone was here.'

The woman, sitting very erect, did not speak.

'I made a fool of myself just now, going arse over—'

The woman remained silent.

'I apologise for disturbing your deliberations.'

She still did not move.

'Isn't it a bit late for it?'

The woman made the merest hint of movement, her face turning a fraction in his direction.

'It's never too late for justice, in this world or the next,' she said drily.

'Ah. I see what kind of judge you are. You believe there'll be a next world.'

'And I know what kind of human being you are. You believe justice can be escaped.'

'Many people escape justice. In fact, all the powerful people I know have escaped justice.'

'Is that why you hound the powerless and celebrate the powerful?'

'What?'

'Have you ever done anything that wasn't in your own interest?'

'Who are you?'

'Have you ever done anything for anyone else?'

'Are you here for the festival?'

'No.'

'So, who are you, then? This is a private party—'

'Why have you attacked so many people's private lives?'

'I beg your pardon—'

'You are not pardoned.'

'Do I know you?'

'I hope not.'

'What does that mean?'

'Da: Dharma. Who have you helped?'

'What do you mean? Who sent you?'

There was a long pause. The woman did not answer. But she turned another fraction of a degree in his direction. She was still in silhouette. Something in her posture stopped him coming closer. He stood, wavering.

'Madame Sosostris has sent me to ask you a question.'

'Charlatans only give answers.'

'Her answer depends on yours.'

'I would like it to be stated, so we're clear about it, that I don't believe in what she does. What's her question?'

There was another long pause.

'She sent me to ask you—'

'So she's not coming to the party?'

'That depends on you.'

'On me?'

'She sent me—'

'What's your name?'

The woman's voice displayed great patience.

'Mrs Equitone.'

'A nice name for a judge who goes about her work at midnight. I didn't know judges and fortune tellers colluded. It confirms my suspicion that justice is a loaded game of chance.'

'You think the justice system is a lottery?'

'The weak are punished, the powerful escape. The wealthier you are the less tax you pay. The poorer you are the more they take from you.'

'You think the rich escape justice?'

'Of course. A billionaire attempts to overthrow the government and a year or two later he's back running for high office. A poor man gets caught with a stick of marijuana, and he's jailed for eight years. What does that look like?'

'No one escapes justice. They only escape the law. Justice is eternal.'

'So you're not a justice of the law?'

'No.'

There was another pause. Stephen looked around, feeling in some mysterious way cornered.

'What's the question?'

'Madame Sosostris wants to know if you will take her place at the card reading this evening.'

Stephen backed off.

'You're joking.'

'I'm as serious – as an astronaut.'

'Take her place? Me? Make fake prophecies?'

'They won't be fake.'

'If I'm not her, they will be fake.'

'Madame Sosostris will find a way to speak through you.'

'I don't want to be a fortune teller's mouthpiece.'

'But you don't mind being a political party's mouthpiece.'

'That's different.'

'You'd be channelling her.'

'Can't think of anything more reprehensible.'

'You channel many views through your magazine. I thought you'd be comfortable with the concept.'

'What do you know about my magazine?'

'Only that it is highly regarded and failing.'

'And so you want me to impersonate a quack?'

'Your wife doesn't think she's a quack.'

'My wife has all kinds of thoughts. She's entitled to them. I'd rather have my fortune told by a donkey. I'd rather be dragged by a hundred horses than do this.'

'Not even to save your fortunes?'

'I can save my fortunes myself.'

'One last try,' said the woman, turning her profile a little more towards him. 'Won't you do this for a friend?'

'Not if it means supporting something I find dubious. Forecasting the future.'

'Your magazine forecasts the future all the time. You forecasted all kinds of futures before the last election. You hire journalists to make predictions.'

'Predictions informed by data—'

'Data can be interpreted a thousand ways. The past is no guide to the future.'

'Is Madame Sosostris a better guide?'

'You look to the past, which is unclear and partial, like the face of the moon.'

'And Madame Sosostris?'

'She looks into all time. Which is here.'

'I don't see it,' Stephen said, looking round.

'How like you to try to see time. Time is not real, but all time is here.'

'I hate paradoxes.'

'So, you won't do it?'

'I won't give legitimacy to a fraud.'

The woman rose.

'Do me a favour,' she said. 'Keep our words to yourself.'

Then she turned and walked briskly back into the woods.

'Wait!' cried Stephen. 'Who are you?'

He ran after her only to come back a few moments later.

'She's gone. It's almost as if she was never here.'

Then for the first time he heard the tones of a new music drifting gently on the wind.

4

Viv and Beatrice were in a changing room in the old stables. They had piled assorted costumes on chairs and around the room and were rifling through them.

Beatrice pulled out a red cassock and held it against her body. Then she picked out a sparkling emerald tiara.

Viv's attention was captured by a magician's cape, black and velvet with a sequined pentagram on the back. She waved the accompanying wand in the air.

'I feel like Merlin,' she said.

'You seem to have raided a whole costume department,' Beatrice laughed.

'It was a stick'em up job.'

'I'm still not sure I can do this.'

'Of course you can,' said Viv. 'You always think you can't do things and then you do them more brilliantly than anybody.'

'This is different. I can do anything if I've got some experience in it. I can run charities, campaign for elections. But be an actor, take on another personality, that's beyond me. And as for telling fortunes? I can't see beyond the end of my nose. Everyone knows I'm the worst forecaster. If I look at the sky and say it's not going to rain, it's definitely going to bucket cats and dogs and rabbits. I have absolutely no talent at prognostication.'

'What a good word!'

'Isn't it? Proud of myself for using it. Thing is, though, if I could have actually seen into the future, I would have avoided so much anguish.'

'But you don't have to see into the future, Beatrice. You just have to see the present.'

'I can't do it. Even thinking about it makes me come out in hives. Have you seen the folk out there, the festival-goers? They're wild. How am I supposed to manage them?'

'Just say what comes into your mind. Free associate.'

'Why don't you do it yourself? You're better at these things than me. You're a good forecaster.'

'And I'm forecasting now.'

'Seriously, you've got the personality for it. You've got authority. I don't.'

'Fiddlesticks! Crises bring out hidden talents. And this is definitely a bloody crisis.'

'Look at me! I'm shaking. It's like before a big date.'

'Don't remind me. I went to the little girl's room five times before I could face my first date. Then I spilled tea all over his crotch.'

'Did he get the message?'

'Message?'

'That you wanted to do something hot.'

'He was livid. A bit of a frozen fish.'

'Hence the hot tea.'

'Said we weren't destined for one another.'

'Which you weren't.'

'No, thank God. He ran off with a mousy girl and bullied her for the rest of his life.'

'Spilling the tea on him, that was prognostication.'

They both laughed.

'You can do this,' Viv said. 'Practise on me.'

'Now?'

'Why not? I've got a deck of cards to hand somewhere.'

'What did you bring those for?'

'They always come in handy.'

Viv got out the cards and gave the pack to Beatrice.

'Pretend you're a wise old gypsy. I've come for a reading.'

Beatrice composed herself for a moment. When she spoke her voice had a gypsy timbre.

'What would you like to know, my child?'

Viv entered into the spirit.

'I want to know if I will be happy in love.'

Beatrice shuffled the pack.

'Take two cards,' she said in the same quivering voice. 'Put them on the table, face up.'

Viv did so, trying to suppress a giggle.

'One more.'

Viv took another. Beatrice studied them.

'It's not looking good. Not good at all. You picked The Lovers, upside down—'

'Upside down?'

'Don't interrupt.'

'Oh, sorry,' said Viv, taken aback by Beatrice's change of tone.

'Upside down, The Lovers mean a break up, or they mean someone is going to cheat, or someone is already cheating. Who is this? You?'

'What?'

'Maybe you cheat with your work. Maybe you are married to work not to your man. Give work all your love, and give man nothing.'

'What are you talking about?'

'Second, you pick The Devil. Why? You make deal with the devil? Is that why you are so successful? You sell your soul to be in House of Lords—'

'Stop,' Viv said. 'Not cool. Not funny.'

She snatched up the cards. Beatrice stared at Viv as if from far away. Then she blinked.

'The third card you chose—'

'Stop!'

'What's the matter?'

'What were you doing?'

'When?'

'Just now.'

'I was doing the reading.'

'Was that you talking?'

'When?'

'Just now.'

'What do you mean?'

'Alright. *Basta*. I get the picture.'

'What picture?'

Viv gave Beatrice a look.

'Okay, we'd better go. They need to announce that Madame Sosostris is here.'

'Is she?' said Beatrice, looking around.

5

WORD WAS SENT out for the revellers to congregate in the open grounds where the tents had been erected and where the piano glistened in the dark beneath the sycamore tree. And from the far corners of the extensive grounds, from the cornices of the château to the overhanging leaves of the casuarina trees, from the dense woods in which dim forms whispered, to the orangery where giant orchids flowered, the revellers were summoned.

Some of them came in small groups. Some walked alone in their rustling costumes. Ghostly forms drifted through the begonias and canna lilies. Voices whispered in the saffron wind, sibilant like ancient priestesses of Apollo speaking through portals at Delphi. Sometimes the voices sounded like bats at twilight. A dense fragrance of rose accompanied the forms as they came from remote corners of the *domaine*. They congregated round a white piano that someone had brought out into the grounds. A pianist in a double-faced mask, dressed like a magician, with a mantle and a white cord, was liberating Debussy preludes with expressive fingers. Looked at from the back the pianist seemed to be facing the audience. But from the front the masked figure played with dreamy abandon. The revellers settled themselves into a moonlit reverie. There was a sword on the piano, and a wand on the pianist's lap. As they played, the pianist spoke.

'You all know why you're here.'

There was a pause while the wind whispered.

'Maybe you don't.'

The wind sighed.

'But you all accepted the invitation.'

Another pause.

'You all have one thing in common.'

'What?' the revellers shouted back.

'We won't speak about it.'

'Why not?'

'Because we're here to forget. And so I play you the music of forgetfulness, the music of moonlight.'

Another pause.

'Why are we all here?'

'To forget,' cried the revellers in one voice.

'And what do we want to forget?'

'That we are unhappy,' they cried.

Then the performer began to improvise, moving so far from the melody that it left its original key, became stretched and strained and broken, like the faraway lament of foxes, or of lonely cats in alleys, or of cracked souls sighing in the black wind. Monumental chords rose like waves on a monstrous sea, then crashed back down to the home keys of *Clair de lune*, bringing back its light enchanted mood, like a cooling breeze on hot skin.

'I have an announcement to make,' the performer said, gently this time.

'There isn't going to be a fortune teller,' one of the revellers called out. 'We've heard that already.'

The performer elaborated on the Debussy theme, wandering off to distant keys, till the music bore no resemblance to itself at all, sounding now like something snatched from a raw wind.

The festival-goers were growing restless.

'The music is sounding sinister,' said one.

'But more beautiful. It fills me with sadness,' said the second.

'The melody stole upon us in the woods,' said the third. 'And it drew us here.'

'That piano is enchanted,' said the first.

'The pianist is changing before our eyes,' said the second.

'They're not changing. We are,' said the third. 'That music is doing stuff to us.'

'I feel heartbreak pouring out of that piano.'

'I feel the misery of someone who was in love but not loved in return. Someone abandoned—'

'I feel the agony of lonely nights, pining for a lover who's gone, who's married someone else, who's never going to return.'

'I hear obsession—'

'I hear confusion—'

Suddenly, with a loud bang, the music stopped. The listeners, collectively, cried out. The pianist stared at them, as if they were bathed in a spectral light.

'I have an announcement to make. Defying all obstacles, the fortune teller is here.'

'Hurray!' cried one of the revellers.

'At last!' cried another.

'Now maybe something interesting will happen,' said a third.

'My beloved might come back. The cards could foretell it.'

The performer interrupted them.

'Make your way to the pavilion at the top of

the hill, form a queue, if you please, in an orderly manner—'

Each one wanted to be the first in the line. A mild, polite scramble ensued. Then the piano began again the poignant melody of heartbreak.

6

Something was moving in the woods.

Alan stumbled into a clearing, pulling vines and burrs off his clothes. Then Stephen staggered out, nearly falling over him. They stopped and glared at each other.

'Venetian clown?'

'Something like that. Toulouse Lautrec?'

'At your service. Have you seen my wife anywhere?'

'No, I haven't. Have you seen mine?'

'We can't both have lost our wives.'

'I spoke to someone I thought was my wife, but she wasn't.'

'I spoke to someone who I thought wasn't my wife, and she was.'

There was a pause.

'Do you know what I dread most?' said Alan.

'Finding out that your wife doesn't love you?'

'No, though I often suspect it.'

'What husband doesn't?' said Stephen.

'I thought you intellectual types were more secure.'

'I catch a faraway look in her eyes sometimes—'

'Yeah, that faraway look.'

'It gives me troubling thoughts.'

'Best not to probe.'

'I wonder, is she remembering some fling?'

'A youthful orgy.'

'A boyfriend who did things to her.'

'Some holiday in the sun when she—'

'Best not to speculate,' said Stephen. 'What is it you dread, then?'

'That you-know-who might be coming.'

There was a pause.

'Madame Sosostris? She had some bad news and isn't coming. Fancy a fortune teller not being able to tell their own—'

'I knew an astrologer whose wife was cheating on him. Why couldn't he read that in the charts?'

'I knew a healer who was always getting a cold.'

'My dermatologist had a bad skin condition for years. It gives you no confidence.'

'I had a banker friend who was always asking me for a loan.'

'Did you give him one?'

'At the highest rate of interest. He still hasn't paid me back.'

'I knew a mechanic whose car kept breaking down.'

'I knew a poet who never had a pen on him. Was always borrowing mine. Made you wonder—'

A tickle of music could almost be heard from the direction of the château, indistinguishable from the sound of the wind through the bamboo trees on the edge of the woods.

'Beatrice, my wife,' began Stephen, 'has taken to surrounding herself with quacks. The other day a strange woman filled the house with crystals. You couldn't sit on a sofa without getting your bottom pierced. It was supposed to improve the feng shui.'

'Probably improved the feng shui of your anal passage. Can you imagine my wife has taken up yoga? Contorting herself!' said Alan. 'I mean, she's in the House of Lords, for chrissake!'

'Ghastly! I tried it once, couldn't unravel myself for days.'

Another pause.

'Then came Madame Sosostris,' continued Stephen.

'The Famous Clairvoyant.'

'The weirdest woman in Europe.'

'I thought she was the wisest.'

'I've never believed in the cards,' said Stephen.

'Or the tarot.'

'Or the crystal ball.'

'Or the charts.'

'What does it say in *Hamlet*? "Springes to catch woodcocks."'

'Precisely,' said Alan.

'The only fortune-telling I believe in,' said Stephen emphatically, 'is hard bloody work.'

'The only fortune-telling I believe in is good old-fashioned reason.'

'Beatrice believes there's a limit to what reason can do.'

'But reason has done everything,' said Alan.

'She believes in intuition. She's reading Kant.'

'Kant and astrology? Peculiar mix.'

'Why do you dread Madame Sosostris so much?'

'They say she can see things. They say it's quite uncanny.'

'You don't believe all that, do you?'

'No. But— what if they're right? Could turn everything upside down.'

'We all fear what we can't control.'

'What we don't understand.'

'Scrying with mirrors.'

'The world of spirits,' said Alan

'Séances.'

'Crystal balls.'

'Talking to the dead.'

'Meddling with charts.'

'Fiddling with the future.'

'One can never be too careful. What if she really sees stuff? What if she messes with the future?' Alan said, almost in a whisper.

'You scared of the future?'

'Not the future. But this moment. Standing on a ledge. The sheer drop before you. The abyss behind you.'

'Let's face it, we can't know the future.'

'But do we really know the past?'

'And the present?'

'That's the great mystery,' said Alan, looking towards the stables.' I'm relieved that sybil isn't coming.'

'The last sybil was caged in Rome. There's a useless fact.'

'Not so useless. The last sybil simply failed to show up.'

'I better go and find my wife, or it'll be the end of me.'

'I better go and find mine before she starts imagining things.'

They paused and cocked their ears.

'I can hear that piano again,' said Stephen. 'Music to wake the dead.'

'Don't talk about the dead,' said Alan, shivering.

'You, afraid of ghosts? Don't make me laugh.'

'You think you're the only sensitive person around here?'

'You're about as sensitive as a wolf.'

'And you – what do you think you are? Just because you own a—'

'I'm not listening. I'm going to look for my wife.'

'I'm going to look for my wife.'

They both stood a moment, listening to the music of the distant piano. Then they went off in opposite directions.

7

ALAN TRAMPED THROUGH the trees, fuming. Walking one path, then another. Feeling lost, he shouldered his way through a mass of vines and came upon a woman. She was in an elegant costume, but her mask was lowered. At first Alan didn't recognise her. But then he went towards her and spoke.

'Why did you bring me to this godforsaken event?'

'What do you mean?'

'You dragged me to this horror show.'

'What're you talking about?'

'I'm fed up.'

'You're fed up? I'm fed up.'

'What are you fed up with?'

'You. Your moodiness, your sulkiness, your constant carping.'

'I don't carp.'

'It's your favourite fish.'

'Well, you seem to think being in the House of Lords has actually made you a baroness.'

'You seem happy to rub your nose in the trough when it suits you.'

'I do nothing for myself. Most of my money is sunk in your good causes. Like this one.'

'You didn't put a penny in.'

'I did.'

'You'll get every penny back in tax rebates. You never do anything for nothing.'

'Why should I?'

'What's really eating you?'

'Your schemes, your bonkers ideas.'

'It's really about you, though, isn't it? You want to be someone else, someone you can't be.'

'Me? Who do I want to be?'

'I don't know. Maybe someone more intellectual, like Stephen.'

'Stephen? That simpering specimen—'

'At least he's honest about himself.'

'What am I not honest about?'

'What you want.'

'What on earth does that mean?'

'I wanted to be in the House of Lords. For all sorts of reasons. I got there. I wanted this festival—'

'And it's a failure. Madame Sosostris isn't coming.'

'I can't have it fail.'

'What, you're too big to fail? Look, Viv, everyone fails some time.'

'But not me. Because, if I fail, the House of Lords fails. Democracy fails.'

Alan stared at her.

'Aren't you being absurd?' he said quietly.

'How little you understand the way the world works,' Viv replied.

'But the world is rational!' shouted Alan. 'It doesn't listen to fortune tellers or quacks like that.'

'Alan, you don't know what anything really is. Reality is not rational. You've imposed your version of rationality on the world and expect it to behave that way.'

'Well, good luck,' Alan laughed. 'Good luck getting Sosostris at your party. All dressed up and nowhere to go.'

Then he tramped back into the woods.

8

IN ANOTHER PART of the forest, Stephen was struggling to extricate himself from clinging vines. When he got free he stumbled into a clearing, where he found Beatrice, taking a breather. Her mask was in her hand.

'Just who I was looking for,' he said, lowering his own. 'I'm never doing this again.'

'What?'

'Leaving myself open to such disrespect.'

'What?'

'Why are we even here?'

'We?'

'Why am I here, then? I'm fed up with being an ornament. I come to these things. I support you. And for what?'

'You never minded before.'

'I do now.'

'Have you been having words with Alan?'

'What do you mean "words"?'

'Whenever you men get together you reinforce the worst in each another.'

'That's exactly what I think when you women get together. You're always slightly less likeable afterwards.'

'And you're much less yourself afterwards.'

'Meaning?'

'You want to be more like Alan.'

'That ape neck—'

'You envy his masculinity.'

'Is that what you call it? Well, since we're being frank, it seems to me that you want to be Viv. You want her influence, her money, her—'

'Actually, women are more realistic about these things than men. I admire what she is. But why should I be jealous of her? My envy, as you put it, is really admiration. I'd like to be more like her, but I accept what I am and I'm fine with it. Also, I'll never forgive you for saying that, even if it is true.'

'You're pissed off because I saw through your facade?'

Beatrice smiled.

'You never understood art. Why do you think Diana turned Actaeon into a stag and set his own dogs on him?'

'Because he saw her naked.'

'No. It's because he didn't know when it was wise not to see.'

Beatrice looked at him a moment. Then she left.

9

Stephen found a path less cluttered with vines and was about to get out of the clearing, when Alan suddenly appeared.

'What have you been saying to my wife?' he shouted.

'What have you been saying to mine?'

'That's the trouble with you bookish types. You can't just come out and say what's on your mind. You have to be sneaky about it—'

'You think your money gives you the right to say whatever you want.'

'It does! That's why I work so hard. I want to do whatever I want.'

'But you don't, do you? You do what Viv wants.'

'Say that again!'

Stephen laughed.

'In Latin or Greek or French or Italian? Which?'

'I hire people like you and fire them three months later just for kicks.'

'I know stuff about you that you can't buy off me for anything.'

'Maybe I should buy your magazine, and hire you to edit it.'

'I've heard you're nothing like as rich as you say. Does your wife know you're in debt?'

'I'm refinancing.'

'Is that what you call it?'

'What do you know about money?'

'I'm not trying to pass as something I'm not.'

'I've earned what I have. I fought for it.'

'With your wife's connections.'

'Nobody speaks about my wife—'

They grappled. In the midst of the struggle they heard the music in the distance suddenly grow louder. The haunting notes of a piano stopped them in their fight. They straightened themselves up and fixed their clothes.

'Sounds like Madame Sosostris is here,' Stephen said.

'I'm not getting a reading.'

'Me neither.'

'Want to grab a drink?'

'Brilliant idea,' said Stephen.

They staggered out of the woods together.

BOOK FOUR

1

AT THE SUMMIT of the hill there was the white pavilion. Above the entrance to the pavilion there was a printed legend:

Madame Sosostris
Famous Clairvoyant
You can't be too careful these days

Inside the tent sat Beatrice, still in her Joan of Arc costume, listening to the clamour of voices outside. She had taken a peek earlier and seen the ghostly forms climbing up the hill, forming a long queue that stretched down into the enchanted woods. She could hear their nasal murmuring. Their words sounded as though filtered through underwater caverns. Above their voices floated thin skeins of the piano music that had haunted the evening. Sometimes it was forlorn, then bright and brilliant, then Arabic, laced with lament and laughter.

2

BEATRICE SET ABOUT becoming Madame Sosostris. She was systematic about it because she knew it would take a long time. First she peeled off her Joan of Arc costume. Then she put on the one that she and Viv had pulled together from the scraps in the suitcase, an embroidered silk midnight blue gown, a velvet cape, and on her head a satin headwrap, with a black lace mantilla, and a mother-of-pearl-coloured veil. Dangling from her ears were moon-shaped earrings. A ring with a blue pyramid on it now adorned one hand.

She elongated the form of her eyebrows, put some dark bronzer on her cheeks, and stuck a mole on her chin. Then she drew the lightest, barest suggestion of a third eye in the middle of her forehead. If you weren't looking for it, you wouldn't see it. But it would be there.

Horus eyes were displayed about the tent along with printed alchemical symbols for gold and for the sun, for the quintessence and for mercury. A pentagram hung just above her seat and a generally occult atmosphere was created with the discreet diffusion of rose incense.

A curtain of fine gauze hung between Madame Sosostris's chair and the client's. The lighting was subdued. It made Beatrice feel bigger and more mysterious. She had practised the voice and had found the effect she desired. It would be deep and resonant.

By the time she finished, Beatrice had disappeared completely. She looked at herself in the mirror and winked. Her eyes, ringed with kohl, had an enigmatic force.

On the table before her was a pack of tarot cards. Plangent notes glided into the tent.

She was ready. She cleared her throat and sat up, a picture of power, staring straight ahead as if she could pierce the thoughts of anyone who came before her, as if she could see the mingled tragedy and comedy of their lives. If she had come in to have her cards read, Beatrice would not have recognised herself.

3

In a clear, bold voice Beatrice, as Madame Sosostris, addressed the opening in the tent.

'COME IN, IF you want your destiny revealed!'

The first visitor walked in backwards, a dim masked figure in a pristine white suit.

'Don't be afraid, my child,' said Madame Sosostris. 'Sit down.'

'There's a queue going all the way down the hill,' said the person in white.

'So many?' said Madame Sosostris calmly. 'I did not know that love had undone so many.'

'That's why we're all here.'

'I know. Sit down.'

There was a short pause, as the visitor sat down.

'I sense about your past a lot of water,' said Madame Sosostris. 'You were drowning—'

The visitor became agitated.

'How true! How true!' said the first visitor. 'You deserve the reputation you have among the dead.'

'Tell me about it.'

'I was on a cruise when my life fell apart. I discovered, quite by accident, or maybe not, the photograph of another woman in my husband's pocket. She was very beautiful. I showed it to him and he started to laugh, and while he laughed he confessed.'

She paused.

'Blinded by grief, by jealousy, I threw myself into the sea.'

She paused again.

'I couldn't swim. I could hear his laughter as I drowned. I hear it still. It accompanies my eternal dreams.'

There was a long silence.

'What do you want to know?' asked Madame Sosostris.

'I want to know if my past could have been different.'

Madame Sosostris looked at her coolly, then shuffled the cards. She laid them out fan-wise on the table.

'Pick three cards.'

The visitor picked three cards and gave them to Madame Sosostris, who placed them face upward,

146

in a line, one after the other, on the table. She laid them out ceremoniously, with an elegant movement of her wrist and a kind of nonchalance. Then she inspected them.

'I see,' she said.

'What do you see?'

'You have chosen The Lovers, Temperance, and The Drowned Phoenician Sailor.'

'What do they mean?'

'You wish to alter your past?' said Madame Sosostris, speaking in a voice that felt as if it came from somewhere behind her.

'Yes.'

'Why?'

'So my death may be different.'

'You don't like your death?'

'I wish I'd had a better one. The one I had gives me no rest. I dwell in endless torment. I wish for release.'

'You can only alter your past by altering your future,' said Madame Sosostris flatly.

'How do I do that?'

'You have to boil your past in the petals of red roses that eyes have not gazed upon.'

'Where I dwell there are many such roses.'

'Your past would have been different if you had tempered your ardour at the beginning.'

'Tempered my ardour?' said the visitor, surprised. 'But I was madly in love with him.'

'You threw yourself into love as into a fire.'

'The sea was a fire.'

'You should have gone more slowly. The slower burns longer.'

'I wish I had been wiser at the beginning,' said the visitor sadly.

'I wish you had also been wiser at the end,' responded Madame Sosostris. 'Our ends alter our beginnings.'

The visitor rose, sensing that the consultation was over.

'Thank you for putting my heart at rest,' she said. 'I will correct my past. I will liberate my death. Can I give you a token?'

'If you wish,' said Madame Sosostris, drawing back. 'What is it?'

'The photograph of the woman who ruined my life.'

The first visitor placed the photograph on the table, then bowed and left, her eyes fixed on the horizon.

4

MADAME SOSOSTRIS STUDIED the photograph in silence for a while then tucked it away in the box beside her chair. She put the cards back into the deck.

The second visitor entered, walking sideways.

'Sit down, my child,' said Madame Sosostris. 'You have nothing to fear.'

'I have everything to fear,' said the visitor in a quivering voice.

'Why is that?'

'My errors are all around me.'

'Sit down,' said Madame Sosostris. Then as the second visitor hesitated, she changed her mind. 'Better still, stand.'

The visitor sat and stood up again hastily.

'I sense much fire in your past. You were burning, but not in flames.'

'How perceptive of you! How true!' cried the

second visitor. 'It is with justification that you are known in our world as the wiliest woman in Europe.'

'Unburden yourself, my child,' said Madame Sosostris, settling into her seat.

The second visitor paused a moment and then launched forward.

'It's painful to remember the truth. Those were the happiest days of my life. I was young, I was gifted, and I had met the love of my life. Because of her, I felt there was nothing I couldn't do.'

There was a pause, as the visitor sobbed.

'Her beauty often made me weep.'

He bowed his head for a moment.

'But she was ambitious and calculating and cold.'

Another silence, as he lifted his head to the light.

'I came home early one day and caught her in bed with her boss. His huge wristwatch was on the bedside table. It was an electronic watch, but I could hear it ticking. I think I went mad. I locked the doors and set the house on fire and let all of us burn. I could hear the ticking of his watch as we burned to death. The sound accompanies me in the long twilight of the empty world.'

'What do you want to know?' asked Madame Sosostris, straightening her neck.

'I want to know whether my past could have been sweeter. Could I have made her love me more?'

Madame Sosostris shuffled the cards and laid them on the table, fan-wise.

'Pick three cards.'

The second visitor picked three cards and gave them to Madame Sosostris. She lay them on the table.

'How fascinating,' she said.

'What do you see?'

'You have chosen The Chariot, The Lovers, and The Tower.'

'What do they mean?'

'Do you wish to make your past better?'

'I feel now that I had many possible futures, but chose the wrong one. I am haunted by the life that I did not live, a life in which I could have been happy. This thought gives me no peace. I live in the inferno of perpetual regret and crave liberation.'

'Your life can only be better if you become simpler. Your future is fixed, but your past can be remade.'

'How?'

'You have to regenerate your past with the incense of meditation, incense that has not been made with the hands of the living,' said Madame Sosostris.

'Where I dwell such incense makes our insomnia bearable. I didn't know it had other uses.'

'Many things in the universe have unexpected uses,' said Madame Sosostris.

She paused a moment.

'Your past could have been better if you had not let yourself be deceived by yourself.'

'But I was deceived by another.'

'She deceived you because you had already deceived yourself into thinking that she loved you.'

'I believed she loved me. I saw many proofs of it.'

'You saw things the wrong way round. You didn't look below the surface.'

'When I looked below the surface, what I saw destroyed me.'

Madame Sosostris didn't speak for a moment. And when she did it was with a lighter voice.

'You gave the reins of your chariot to someone else.'

'What should I have done?'

'Listened to your soul, not to your eyes.'

The second visitor rose, sensing that his time with the famous clairvoyant was ending.

'Thank you for showing me to myself. I will adjust my past. I will transform my death. Can I give you a token?'

'If you wish,' said Madame Sosostris. 'What is it?'

'The watch she gave me. It stopped working the exact moment she broke my heart.'

The second visitor placed the watch on the table, bowed politely, and departed.

5

MADAME SOSOSTRIS LOOKED at the watch for a moment, gave a shudder, and put it away. She rearranged the cards, smoothed her garments, and waited for the third visitor, who soon glided in.

'Sit, my child,' said the famous clairvoyant.

'Thank you.'

Madame Sosostris suddenly noticed something.

'Send away the others.'

The visitor looked round.

'What others?'

'All around you,' Madame Sosostris said, waving at the air around the third figure. 'You have brought legions with you.'

She paused.

'Send them away!'

The visitor looked about and at first saw nothing.

But then she began to shoo away a host of imaginary people.

'Go away, all of you!' she cried. 'Leave me alone! Night and day, asleep or awake, you never leave me alone. Go away!'

Madame Sosostris smiled.

'That's right,' she said. 'You can only come here on your own. You can only face yourself alone.'

'I've been too much alone since—'

'But not alone enough.'

At Madame Sosostris's invitation, the visitor sat down.

'Unfold yourself, my child,' she said.

The third visitor composed herself. Then she began.

'I was the happiest of people. I was always laughing. I had a talent for the stage. I brought joy. Maybe I was unstable and didn't know it. Then something blasted my life all to pieces. I fell passionately in love. I wish to forget them but cannot forget. Oh, curse the memory!'

She paused.

'I loved them with the fullness of the sea, the simplicity of a child, the innocence of a flower, the sweetness of a nightingale.'

She paused again, struggling with her emotions.

'I couldn't live without them. I needed to hear their voice, to feel their eyes on me, touch their skin.'

She paused, slightly longer this time.

'Then one day they walked out of my life.'

A shorter pause.

'Leaving me a letter.'

Another pause, accompanied by a movement of the hand.

'I read that letter a thousand times. Through tears. I read it till I thought the note was saying the opposite of what it said.'

A sniffle followed.

'Soon I was showing everyone the note. I wanted them to see how greatly I was loved, how loving they were to me. I showed the note to people whose eyes were empty, who did not see what I saw. I have been living among those people ever since. They grow in number, clustering about me, jealous of my note, envious of my love. Never alone, always alone. With the note that I can only read through tears.'

When she'd finished she was silent.

'What do you want to know?' the celebrated fortune teller asked after a pause.

The visitor took her time.

'Could I have done something that would have made them stay? Could I have inspired a loving note, if I had lived in a different way?'

Madame Sosostris shuffled the cards and laid them on the table slowly.

'Pick three cards.'

The third visitor picked three cards and gave them to Madame Sosostris. She laid them in a semi-circle on the table. The fabled clairvoyant inspected the cards.

'How strange!' she said.

'What?'

'You have chosen The Hierophant, The Hermit, and Justice.'

'What do they mean?'

'You wish to make your past happier?' asked Madame Sosostris.

'I think now that I had many pasts. Each one could have led to a different future. I had all the gifts, all the imagination. As it was, my life was reduced to a single note, from which I seek redemption.'

'Your past would have been different if you had listened to yourself. You have already made your future with your own hands, but your past can be redeemed,' said Madame Sosostris.

'My past wasn't made with my hands but with my heart. How could I not follow my heart?' said the figure, her voice thinning.

Madame Sosostris made her first mildly impatient gesture.

'Was it really your heart you followed, or the weakness of your mind? Whenever people want to avoid responsibility for their decisions in life they say they were following their heart. We listen to a wrong impulse and we call it the heart. You malign the heart when you blame it for every stupid decision you make.'

'How can I learn to listen to my heart?' asked the third figure, a little contrite.

'That is an inward discipline. Go into the silence and listen. Use what is left of your brief eternity to cultivate the art.'

'How can my past be redeemed?'

'You must rewrite your life with a pen made from the feathers of the Phoenix, the ink from the tears of one who has never lied, and paper made with laughter.'

'Such things are rare where I live,' said the third figure. 'But they can be acquired.'

Madame Sosostris picked up the three cards again.

'Your past would have been magical if you had listened to what you knew in your bones to be true.'

'Now the winds of fate blow through my bones.'

There was a pause. Madame Sosostris spoke again.

'You had a special path ahead of you, leading to a high hill. You could have climbed high and been a light to the world, if you had not lost your way.'

There was silence for a moment. Then the visitor gave a short, almost hysterical laugh.

'It's so easy to lose one's way when one looks at the world with wrong eyes.'

Madame Sosostris was still looking at the three cards. Then she made a noise like her breath catching in her throat.

'The strange thing,' she said, 'is that you did not get what you deserved. You read the note the wrong way. If you had read it the right way, your pain would have been brief, and you would have drawn new motivation from it, and your life would have found its destiny on the high hill.'

The visitor rose, feeling that her time with the legendary fortune teller was at an end.

'Thank you for teaching me to trust myself. I feel lighter already. I will redeem my past. Can I leave you a token?'

'If it pleases you,' said Madame Sosostris. 'What is it?'

'The thing that keeps me trapped in misery. By giving it to you I will free myself from this gloom. I set free all the dismal companions that accompany me.'

'What is it?'

'The note that cracked the music of my heart.'

The third visitor left the handwritten note on the table, and bowed. On light feet she departed.

Madame Sosostris read the note, and sighed.

6

MADAME SOSOSTRIS SAT listening to the wispy notes of the distant piano. She needed a moment to recover.

Since the third visitor left, many more had passed through the tent, bringing with them their griefs and sorrows, stories that quivered with horror, blood-curdling acts of revenge, and terrible deaths. They had all been driven, all haunted, by the infernal powers of love.

The visitors brought harrowing tales of abandonment, of betrayal, of cold-hearted rejection. Madame Sosostris had been staggered to hear how people clung to loves that had died, to relationships that were killing them, to marriages that were destroying their souls. She was shocked to learn what people would do to get back the love they had lost, that had abandoned, abused and often defrauded them. Some of the visitors were of this earth and many were not.

After a while she could no longer tell the difference. Love made for them all the same inferno.

With the first visitor she had made an effort to be Madame Sosostris. But by the second something happened. A lightness took over. With the third visitor something like a breeze, a fragrant wind, entered her and worked its way into her brain. From then on she was not herself. She read the cards with an ease that was beyond her. And she spoke to people who brought their grim destinies to her with an authority that she didn't recognise. Strength emanated from her every gesture, from her eyes.

They had come to her weighed down with the burdens of their unendurable agonies. They left with a streak of light in their eyes. They were people who had chewed their innards and devoured their own hearts. They were locked in the narrow space of their beings. They were imprisoned for long periods of time in the hell of their own minds, turning over their agonies till they grew and filled their world. What most of them needed was a glimpse beyond themselves, a glimpse of something real, something with the texture of dry bone, the stench of a dead beetle, the roughness of a cement wall. She intuited this without knowing how.

During the consultations, she was struck by her reading of the cards. She had never noticed the details in them before. There was a world of destinies in those cards. Every one told a hundred stories. A single detail, grasped at the right moment, pried open a tiny crack through which a single shaft of cosmic light could shine. She understood then the force of the tiniest ray of light. Sometimes the light showed in a gesture. Other times it was a word, a word that had been breathed into her mind a moment before it was uttered.

She saw that people are mysteriously assisted as much as they are blocked, helped as much as hindered. It crossed her mind at one point that destiny was not always what it seemed. A rich life contained the seeds of hell, and a miserable life harbours seeds of paradise. There was simply no way to tell which was which. Some inclination made people choose whether to elevate or depress themselves.

While she was both herself and another these insights raced through her. She wished she could have slowed them down.

In an immeasurable pool of exhaustion, she sat listening to the elongated notes of that almost demonic piano playing from beyond the enchanted woods.

7

SHE HAD SAVED the party, Beatrice told herself. The
long line of visitors was gone, and the consultations
were over. She could already hear the birds of dawn.
She was about to stand up and get out of her garments, remove all trace of Madame Sosostris, when
Alan, still dressed as a jester, stumbled into the pavilion, almost tripping over himself. He pulled himself
up with dignity, and planted himself before Madame
Sosostris, a little shaky on his feet.

She looked at him with a mixture of pity and
irony. She quickly pulled her mantilla on again and
sat down, smoothing her dress.

'Sit, my child,' she said, in a low, powerful voice.
'Steady yourself.'

'Is it really you?' Alan said, his eyes widening.
'Me?'

'I heard you weren't coming. I dreaded your coming.'

Madame Sosostris, a little taken aback, kept a calm face.

'Well, here I am,' she said simply.

'The wisest woman in Europe.'

'So they say.'

'Have you recovered from your cold?'

'My cold?'

'You had a bad cold.'

'Never better,' said the soothsayer.

There was an awkward pause as Alan tried to work out what to do next.

'Sit down,' said Madame Sosostris. 'I sense an empty house. Your house is full but crowded with emptiness.'

'What?'

'I sense emptiness in the fullness of your house.'

Alan stared glassily, as if trying to get her into focus.

'I was afraid of you,' he said, collapsing into the chair across from her. 'But you're right. On the surface, my life is a success. I scare everyone. I run a big company. I'm a pillar of society. I hate pillars. I want to be a dome. I should be happy.'

'Are you not happy?' asked Madame Sosostris, leaning forward a little.

'My wife—'

'What about her?'

'I don't recognise her anymore. She's changed.'

'How?' Madame Sosostris said this with more interest than she intended, making Alan jump a little.

'I thought I knew her. But recently she's become someone else. It frightens me.'

'What has she become?' asked Madame Sosostris.

Alan thought for a moment. He evidently found thinking very difficult.

He straightened up with an effort of will.

'I'm not sure,' he said. 'It's hard to say. She seems bigger. She's like a huge tree that's appeared overnight in my garden. A tree that I don't understand.'

'But you still love her?' Madame Sosostris said.

'I did,' Alan said pausing and looking sheepishly at the formidable fortune teller. 'But how can you love what you don't understand?'

A pause loomed like an abyss between them.

'What question do you want to ask?' asked Madame Sosostris.

'I can't change my past,' said Alan. 'I've lived the life I've lived. Or maybe I haven't lived at all. I've lived in the shadow. Can my future be different from the future I was going to have?'

'What are you concerned about?' said Madame Sosostris, leaning forward and shuffling the cards.

Alan opened his mouth, but nothing came out. He seemed paralysed.

'Let the cards speak for you,' Madame Sosostris said. 'Pick three.'

Alan picked the cards and handed them to her. She laid them on the table negligently. Then she gave them a close scrutiny.

'What can you see?'

She looked up at him slowly, portentously.

'You've chosen The Broken Egg, The Devil, and The Builder.'

'Such weird names,' Alan said. 'I've never heard of two of those cards before.'

'A new future requires a new revelation,' said the indomitable Madame Sosostris.

'What do they mean?'

Madame Sosostris continued as if he hadn't spoken.

'For your future to be different, the egg of your life must be broken. Then you must convert your demons into friends. And you must build a home capable of housing the firmament. But first, for a long time, you will live in an empty house, drinking whisky alone.'

'That's harsh. And my wife?'

'She might be the egg you have broken.'

Alan stood up too fast, stumbled, stood again. He felt dizzy.

'I was right to be afraid of you,' he cried, and he ran, shakily, out of the tent.

Madame Sosostris picked up the three cards and turned them over with a pensive look on her face.

8

THE EVENING WAS concentrating its strength around
the pavilion on the hill. A wind full of lost sighs
swirled about it, rattling it from the outside. The land
below was quiet and still. The multitudes that had
poured up the hill had retreated. Their histories were
piled up in all the corners of the tent. Beatrice wasn't
sure if she was simply tired from her long night's
work or whether she was on the verge of grief. She
felt like weeping for a very long time, but she hadn't
been brought up to do anything like that. Her lips
quivered but she fought back the tide.

As she gathered her things she was aware that
something had changed in her. She was no longer
the same person. She started to rise, gathering herself
as if a mountain of lead weighed on her. She felt
burdened with strange knowledge, as old as the
last sybil of Rome. It passed through her mind that

becoming Madame Sosostris had in some way made her Madame Sosostris. How could that be? Then she remembered the sensation of something passing into her at the beginning of the consultations. She had read somewhere that an avatar could enter a body and live inside it, fulfilling its obscure destiny through the living form of the person. Had that happened to her? She doubted it. But the possibility nagged at her. Besides, Madame Sosostris was alive. Could a living person exchange consciousness with another living person? She shook these thoughts from her head as she put the cards back into their box.

Fragments of music travelled across to her. The music didn't sound so forlorn now, only bruised and wounded but still pure. Her thoughts were returning to the familiar. For a moment she thought about what it would be like to be trapped in the persona of Madame Sosostris for the rest of her life. The power, but also the loneliness. An icy hand gripped her heart at the thought of it. Suddenly she wanted to get out of those clothes, free herself from the awful prison of Madame Sosostris's personality. She felt as if she couldn't breathe, as if she were being slowly strangled, and then the sensation became unbearable.

9

SHE WAS ABOUT to rip the mantilla from her head when Stephen, still with his Parisian hat and cane and monocle, strode in and planted himself before her. She gave a start, but quickly pulled herself together.

'What do you want?'

'You didn't expect to see me, did you?'

'I knew you'd be the last,' Madame Sosostris said. 'I've been expecting you.'

'You have?'

'Sit, my child,' said Madame Sosostris, returning to herself. 'Take that seat in the corner.'

Stephen looked at the seat in the corner. Then he tipped over the consultation table.

'I don't believe in all this,' he said. 'Every man makes his own destiny.'

'Every woman too.'

'Precisely. I know you're a sham. My wife believes

in you. She's simple-minded about this kind of thing.'

'Is she?'

'She believes in acupuncture, fairies, ley lines, destiny, helping people who don't want to be helped, singing in choirs. She can't sing to save her life.'

'You don't admire your wife?'

'My wife is a pillar of society,' Stephen said resonantly. 'She's a trustee of many important organisations. She chairs the boards of lots of charities. If you were to meet her in public, in her cream-coloured suit and her blowdry, you wouldn't guess the outlandish things she believes.'

'I sense—'

'You sense nothing. I sense you are a big society fake. All night I've been watching the fools coming up to this pavilion. They leave as if you've shown them the grail, given them the elixir of life. But you don't have the elixir, do you? And there is no grail. It's all a fraud, isn't it?'

'What do you want to know?' Madame Sosostris asked quietly.

'I don't want to know anything. I want to live. I want liberty. I want to be wild and free. I want to be an artist. I want to be irresponsible and happy. I've lived all my life by the rules. Who wrote those rules? Life is a prison. I want to escape. I'm suffocating.

I'm dying. Every day I think my real life is going to begin. I do important things, chair committees, run the magazine, canvas for the party, raise money for charity, but I'm not living. I want to feel the music and the thrill and the fury and the eternity of each moment. I want to be alive in love. I want to live. Can your cards show me how to live?'

'You're drunk!' said Madame Sosostris sternly.

'Drunk? Drunk? Of course I'm bloody drunk! I should have been drunk more often. In veritas vino!'

'You mean the other way round?'

'Out of truth comes drunkenness,' said Stephen. 'The truth will make you drunk. And when you are drunk everything becomes clear. Things are murky because we have not drunk enough. Can your cards show me how to live, O, woman with a wicked pack of cards?'

'We'll see,' said Madame Sosostris calmly.

She opened the pack and shuffled the cards with practised ease.

'Pick three.'

Roughly, almost insolently, Stephen picked three cards from the spread and threw them down in front of her. She straightened them into a line.

'You have picked Durga, Lady of Stone; The Man shaking a Spear; and The Fool,' Madame Sosostris said with a dry smile.

'Ominous,' said Stephen.

'You want to know if they can tell you how to live?'

Stephen stood, a mad light in his eyes, and began waving his arms about.

'I want to live!' he shouted. 'I want to be free. I've never lived a single day in my life. I've been dwelling under a rock. Would that I could do one thing that has an echo in this vast world where time drains everything of its substance. If only, if only I could set my world in order. The nymphs are gone. I hear thunder whispering through the land. What voices it has! Would that I could live one true moment! If only I could visit again the fisher king and ask him why the river's tent is broken—'

At this point Toulouse Lautrec, who had been making wild gestures with his hands, staggered back, clutching at the side of the pavilion. Then the whole structure slowly collapsed about him. But Madame Sosostris stood still in the middle of it all, solid as a marble statue.

10

THEY WERE SITTING on a log near the collapsed tent. Behind them, the forest glowed. Strange lights sparkled among the leaves. The wind was gentle and bore the odour of ancient sycamores. The silence was punctuated by fragments of that music of lost souls who have found a moment in Elysium. Beatrice and Viv seemed to be listening for something, for footsteps which never arrived.

'It lasted the whole night,' Beatrice said quietly.

'The whole night,' echoed Viv.

'I must have listened to a thousand broken hearts, a thousand tales of woe. It was as if hell itself had emptied.'

'I saw the queue curling up the hill,' said Viv.

'It was only when rosy-fingered dawn—'

'Ah, Homer—'

'—stole over the eastern horizon that the last of them crept away—'

'Free of the burden that had haunted them in the greyness of time.'

'You noticed!'

'I came to see you. Even I didn't recognise you.'

'I didn't recognise myself,' said Beatrice, lifting her face to the last trace of moonlight.

'You seemed to be possessed.'

'I was, first by the spirit of Madame Sosostris herself.'

'Who is a fiction—'

'Who is real.'

'You were possessed by the costume.'

'But then I was possessed by the spirit of heartbreak itself.'

'I'm sure you managed to change a lot of lives.'

'The tent is crammed with all the tokens they left behind.'

'What're you going to do with them?'

'I don't know,' said Beatrice. 'But that's not all the long night left me.'

'What else?' asked Viv nervously.

Beatrice shifted on the log. Her voice changed, and her look crossed to the other side of the world. There was weariness in her voice. For the first time it occurred to Viv that the Beatrice she knew had gone. Her voice was different. Was there a touch of Margate about its timbre?

'My husband came to see me right at the end.'

'You mean Stephen?'

'How many husbands do I have?'

Viv gave a half-hearted snort.

'You've changed. You seem capable of anything now. You could have several husbands for all I know.'

'It's a thought.'

'You don't, do you?'

'Of course not.'

'So he came to see you?'

'He didn't recognise me.'

'That's scandalous.'

'Twice in the one night.'

'That's grounds for—'

'Divorce. Absolutely. Why stay married to a man who doesn't recognise you?'

'But surely—'

'It means he only really loves your face, your money, your—'

'What did you say to him?'

'He made a big scene. Brought the house down.'

'The pavilion, you mean.'

'Same thing. Alan came to see me too.'

'My Alan?'

'Yes.'

'He doesn't believe in fortune-telling.'

'He came in his clown's outfit. He wasn't himself.'

'What did you say to him?' asked Viv a little uneasily.

'Only what the cards revealed.'

'What was that?'

Beatrice paused, then she drew a long breath. Her face became pale.

'You know, Viv, complacency's our undoing. We're secure. We have everything. And because of that we're dead. Dead. We don't feel real emotions. We don't suffer. We don't live. Other people do our living for us. We pay nannies to raise our children, drivers to take us where we want to go, servants to cook for us, shrinks to get rid of our guilt, and friends to make us feel that everything we do is right. We consume and consume. We consume other people, we consume the future, we devour the environment. We have it too easy. And we're dead. We think we're lucky, but we're dead.'

'What're you talking about?' said Viv, pulling back.

'After about six hours of listening to those tales of woe, the hidden griefs, the suffering, it dawned on me. We live in fear. We stick in relationships that don't enrich us, that don't let us see the mystery of life. And we do that because we fear being alone, or poor, or unloved. We cling to lies. Perhaps the real truth is in loss, in being broken.'

'Are you mad? Are you suggesting all couples should break up? Lots of people are happy in their lives and their love affairs.'

'I'm not advocating that people should break up unnecessarily.'

'Then what are you advocating?'

'I listened and I heard life speaking. I heard love speaking. The music of loss. Can you hear it?'

Piano notes had been drifting over from the enchanted woods as they talked.

'I don't hear anything,' said Viv.

'My point exactly. The well-fed don't see the starving. Those who suffer are invisible to the happy.'

'Don't avoid the subject. What did you say to Alan?'

'Even when people said they had moved on, and were happy in new relationships, the most real thing about them was their loss, their pain.'

'You're avoiding the subject.'

'It makes the world go round.'

'What has this to do with Alan?'

'If bad relationships don't break up, good ones don't happen. Being rejected, abandoned, makes us human.'

Viv turned away when Beatrice said that, as though she'd received an electric shock. Beatrice didn't notice.

'The Bible tells us that the human story began with a broken relationship.'

'Will it end with revelation?' Viv said quietly.

Beatrice was in full flow.

'Marriages fall apart, religion goes out of fashion, children grow up and fall out with us, siblings become estranged, friends don't speak to each other for decades. Love begins with a burst of hallelujah and ends with the apocalypse. Breaking is what we do. We've even smashed the balance of nature. We're seeking wholeness. That's why we keep looking for love despite the bad choices we make. Alan wanted to know if his future could be different and I told him what the cards said.'

There was silence between them until Viv cried out suddenly.

'You're not even Madame Sosostris! Who gave you the right?'

'You did!'

They stared at one another like two cats about to engage in a fierce brawl.

'You went beyond the limits of the game,' said Viv.

'Did I?'

'The game was for the others. It was never meant to be for us.'

'You wanted Madame Sosostris. You summoned her.'

'I did no such thing!'

'They always say you should be careful what you wish for,' said Beatrice with a sober voice.

'I was only trying to save the festival.'

'And the festival was saved.'

'But at what cost?'

'Even without the cards,' said Beatrice, leaning back, 'Alan knew that the person he loved was no longer there.'

'No longer there?'

'Taken over by another persona.'

'What persona?'

'The terrible persona of truth,' said Beatrice.

There was the sound of a branch cracking not far from them. The noise seemed unusually large in the gloaming. Two people, dressed as courtiers from the sixteenth century, went running past, the man in giggling pursuit of the woman. Viv stared at them, transfixed, long after they had gone.

11

'I'VE NEVER REALLY told you the truth,' Viv said after a while.

'About yourself?'

'Yes. Those two people running past just now brought it back. I blame these woods for everything.'

'These enchanted woods?'

'Yes. Their influence. They make me feel I need to face something that I have never faced before.'

'Go on.'

'Imagine a girl, in love with the brightest boy of the year. Tall, handsome, self-assured. Everyone wanted him. Then one day this boy settled his sleepy eyes on the girl. On me. I went weak at the knees. I was ready to do anything he wanted. He saw that.'

'What then?'

'He did with me whatever he wanted. He flirted with me in public but left the party with someone else. He humiliated me with cutting remarks about my ankles.'

'Your ankles? What's wrong with them?'

'They're fat.'

'They're not. Never have been.'

'He played with me as though I was a rag doll. He mowed his way through all the girls in our set, and the ones right after us. I hung around him like an orphan who had no home to go to.'

'But, why?'

Viv stared at her.

'What do you see?'

'A successful woman, a first-class lady.'

'I'm nothing of the sort. I'm weak, timid, love-lorn, love-broken. A wreck of a woman who's put on a first-class act all her life.'

'What do you mean?'

'Why did I hang around him? I accepted the dreadful things he did to me, day in day out, because I was addicted to humiliation. He got me hooked on it.'

'Isn't that what love does to us?'

'He once asked me to crawl on the floor, in front of the whole college. On my hands and knees.'

'And did you?'

'Twice. All the way along the line and back again. My knees were bruised by the time I'd finished.'

'I can't see you doing that.'

'I did it with my head held high.'

'You're making this up.'

'Once he asked me to take down my knickers—'

'Stop. I don't want to hear any more.'

'When we graduated, I continued to follow him. He'd summon me in the middle of the night. I actually walked six miles through the woods to get to him because he was depressed. I wore him down eventually. Outlasted all the prettier girls, and in the end, I married him.'

'Who was he?'

'If I tell you his name so near these woods, I'm afraid he might materialise. And I don't want that. I married him, nursed him, boosted his confidence and in no time he regained his former glory. He got a job in the City, and went on to mow his way through all the women I knew, including my best friends. Sometimes I thought they were laughing at me, right in my face. But what did I care? I was addicted. I worked for a hedge fund. We made money together. A fortune. And soon we had a fairy tale life. Until he got three different girls pregnant, at the same time. But even then I wouldn't leave him. Then one morning, he left me. He fled with only the shirt on his back and went to live on the coast with the latest woman in his life. Everyone knew, and everyone pitied me, and I don't know how I didn't die of shame.'

'I had absolutely no idea,' stammered Beatrice.

'How could you? I worked hard to bury it. I threw myself into politics. I gave money to good causes. I changed my image. I found another drug, an even more addictive one than shame.'

'What?'

'Power.'

'You're making my head spin.'

'I've been burying my head in the sand. It's time to strip back to the truth. I'm not who I seem to be. Madame Sosostris saw that right away. She sent me on this path to force me to face my true self. That's why she didn't come, why she sent you in her stead. It wasn't fortune-telling I needed, it was self-revelation.'

The two friends sat silently on the log and the wind laden with sighs blew over them.

12

ALAN WAS IN their room in the château, taking off his fool's outfit, when he felt something slip in behind him. He turned and saw Viv. She was out of her costume already. She had put on a simple pair of black trousers, a red blouse, and her hair hung loose and undone.

The rowdy voices outside were calming down. The night's passions were cooling. Alan held the jester's cap in his hands and stared at it.

'You've heard,' he said.

'I've heard nothing. Tell me what you need to.'

'All my life I've been living someone else's idea of a life, someone else's idea of a man. It's easier playing at being a man than being one.'

'Go on.'

'Madame Sosostris stripped the veneer from me.'

'You mean your mask?'

'Whatever you call it. It was important to me. It kept the world out and the chaos in.'

'It kept the truth out.'

'What truth?'

'That you don't really love me. That you're not who you make yourself out to be. That we're bad for one another.'

'Is anybody what they make themselves out to be?' Alan said. 'We're all putting on a front, making it coherent. The world needs coherence or the whole show stops working. I don't know why you're surprised. If you aren't consistently what you appear to be, how do you do business with people? Nobody wants the truth. We want coherence. We want people to be like public buildings, to look the same today as they did yesterday. You want truth? What do you think would happen if public buildings began revealing their truths? The Tower of London, the House of Commons, your beloved House of Lords. Thankfully buildings keep their truth to themselves, as we should.'

'We're not public buildings, Alan.'

'Some of us are. The Royal Family, heads of government, big corporations. Success is a public building. Banks trust solid things, bricks and mortar, land, and gold.'

'Westminster Abbey or the Tower of London, Alan, it doesn't matter what you think you are. We can't go on like this. I may end up alone, but I'd rather be alone than go on living with someone who isn't what he says he is. Do you know who you are?'

'I'm what attracted you in the first place, the confidence I projected, my authority.'

'You projected promises. They've exhausted me.'

'What do you want?'

'I want a human being, not the relentless pursuit of success.'

'You want me to fail then?'

'You'd be more attractive if you did fail sometimes. It would give me a chance to—'

'Gloat?'

'I'd ban that word.'

'Ban words, and soon you ban people.'

'Did you get that from Stephen?'

'Did he get it from me, you mean?'

'Funny how you want to be him and he wants to be you.'

Alan stood up.

'Why would I want to be him?'

Viv laughed.

'It doesn't matter anymore. Being here has made me see that I can't bear to stay with you any longer.'

'Have you lost your mind?'

'Actually, I think I've found it, after all these years. And I'm going to use it. And you're not bullying me anymore.'

'I've never bullied you. You're the one who bullies me. Your peerage, your achievements—'

'Do you remember, years ago, you slapped me because I interrupted you?'

'I don't remember.'

'At the time I thought I deserved it. I hadn't had my dose of humiliation for a while. I missed it.'

'I don't recognise you. You've changed. Are you drunk? Have you got false memory syndrome? Talk to me.'

'No more. It's been a revelation. I feel free.'

'Of the patriarchy, I suppose.'

'Of myself. I've been my own jailer, trying desperately to be a certain kind of person. But it turns out people like me more when I'm not trying. They like me when I'm not pretending. What's more, I like myself too. Do you know, I never really liked myself before? I don't know if it's age, if it's being in these woods, but for the first time in my life I see that I could be perfectly happy in a little room with one or two good friends—'

'You're a people junkie. You need a whole village, not two people.'

'That's who I was before Madame Sosostris. She stripped the veneer from me too,' said Viv.

Then she stood up and walked out of her husband's life.

13

In a room nearby, Beatrice was just beginning to take off her costume when Toulouse Lautrec burst in, still dazed with a mixture of champagne and adrenalin. He stopped when he saw her and pulled himself up to his full height, eyes blazing.

'So you've finally done it,' Beatrice said, calmly taking off one layer of her costume. 'You've literally brought the house down.'

He didn't move or speak for a long moment. Then he began to move towards her, but it was an ill-conceived notion. He tottered, he staggered, and only managed to stop himself from falling by clutching at her.

'Yet again, the woman props up the toppled giant,' said Beatrice.

Toulouse Lautrec sank into a chair. He stared at Beatrice, and made another huge effort.

'I suppose,' he said, 'I've ruined everything.'

'Pretty much.'

'That Madame Sosostris is pretty tiresome. As pious as a secret gambler. Takes herself far too seriously. I'll say one thing for her, though.'

'What?'

'She's extremely sexy.'

'She is?'

'Something about the power of prophecy, about being able to pierce the enigma of destiny with the mere turning of cards. It's unexpectedly arousing.'

'You've gone out of your mind.'

'Probably, and it's been quite the most liberating experience of my life.'

'You've always been proud of your mental control.'

'I've been living in prison all these years. For the first time I feel as if I am standing outside myself, able to see clearly.'

'And what do you see?'

'Me. A right royal fool.'

'Then I've been a fool too, for loving you.'

She paused.

'That's what I want to tell you,' continued Beatrice. 'The person that loved you is here no longer. She's gone.'

He shook his head in an attempt to clear it.

'What's she done?'

'Gone. Left. Madame Sosostris opened her eyes and she saw that she didn't want to live the dim, narrow, regimented life she had been living.'

There was another long pause.

'I'm sorry, Stephen. We may as well begin proceedings for a mutually acceptable separation.'

Still Toulouse Lautrec was silent.

'Did you hear me?'

He began taking off his costume. The top hat was the first to come off. Then the coat. He struggled with that for a moment, until she came over to help him.

'Did you hear me?' she said. 'It's over. I'm leaving.'

He sat down beside her and took her hand as if he was going to pronounce a prognosis.

'You're not going to read my palm, are you? You're not qualified.'

'Aren't I?'

He peered into her hand.

'You are going to leave your husband,' he said, half-slurring, 'you are going to walk out of your old existence, and you are going to begin the most magical chapter of your life.'

He turned over the other hand and looked at the back of it, before turning to the palm and studying it carefully.

'You're going to meet the love of your life. He's

going to be remarkably like your husband – but freer, happier, cheekier, and more fun. With him you will be the woman you've always wanted to be, free and strong, and sexy. This man will love you in ways that your husband never dreamt of, he will find corners of your body bursting with the potential for bliss and corners of your heart ripe with the possibilities of joy.'

'Where will I find a man like that?'

Stephen peered harder into her palm and then at last he looked into her eyes.

'Madame Sosostris tells me that you will find this man in the ruins of a broken pavilion, for it is only among the broken that you find those with the humility and the vision to create a new world.'

Beatrice held his stare.

'In the ruins of a broken pavilion?'

'Yes. Where I believe your husband perished.'

'The broken pavilion. His finest moment.'

'His greatest disaster.'

Beatrice looked into his eyes.

'And I'll find this new man there?'

'The man your husband could never be. The man who will dedicate himself to making you happy.'

'It takes some balls,' Beatrice said, with a slight lilt in her voice, 'to actually bring the house down.'

'You think?'

'And there's nothing sexier than seeing a man make a magnificent fool of himself without losing any of his pizazz.'

'Is that so?'

Beatrice drew closer to him.

'I would be a magnificent fool myself not to snatch this new man out of the very ruins into which the old one plunged himself.'

'Exquisitely put.'

She kissed him.

'I thought so myself,' Beatrice said, before merging her face in his.

14

ALAN AND STEPHEN were sitting on a log at the edge of the woods. They were back in the light summer clothes they arrived in. An expressive melody drifted from the invisible piano. Lights were on in tents all over the grounds. The marquees were silent. The revellers had left behind them the desolate scenes of their revelry. There were empty bottles growing out of the earth. The fairy lights worked erratically, twinkling off and on in highly irregular rhythms.

'I came as two and now I am leaving as one,' said Alan.

'I think I was always one, but now I'm two. My wife is a wonderful mystery to me.'

'We fall in love with a mystery and then we stop seeing her. Madame Sosostris was my undoing.'

'We believe what we are predisposed to believe,'

said Stephen. 'Othello did not have to believe the evidence of the cambric handkerchief.'

'Madame Sosostris showed me my fear, like a rumour from the future.'

'She stripped me of my folly,' said Stephen.

'Our future begins as a rumour and ends as fact.'

'I should have left her my cane as a token. Instead I left her my fall.'

'I should have left my fool's cap. Instead I left her my flight.'

'This is the last of these events I will be attending.'

'Me too. How will you remember it?' asked Alan.

'I will remember the day Madame Sosostris set me free.'

'I will remember the tears of that enchanted piano.'

Coda

Two women were in a room where the light was low and the mood charged. They sat in silence in the dimness of the room. Then the more radiant of the two women spoke.

'Did it work?'

'Better than we expected. They are all facing different directions.'

'None unchanged?'

'They are all as far from what they thought they were as it is possible to be.'

'That's what they wanted.'

'Nothing happens that is not what we want, or what we need, or what we deserve.'

'There's no such thing as chance.'